DETROIT PUBLIC LIBRARY

P9-EEU-820

Two Sides of a Penny

Part 1

BY
Carlton Brown

Chase Branch Library
17731 W. Seven Mile Rd.
Detroit, MI 48235

SEP - - 2015

C.H.

Life Changing Books
Published by Life Changing Books
P.O. Box 423
Brandywine, MD 20613

This novel is a work of fiction. Any references to real people, events, establishments, or locales are intended only to give the fiction a sense of reality and authenticity. Other names, characters, and incidents occurring in the work are either the product of the author's imagination or are used fictitiously, as are those fictionalized events and incidents that involve real persons. Any character that happens to share the name of a person who is an acquaintance of the author, past or present, is purely coincidental and is in no way intended to be an actual account involving that person.
Library of Congress Cataloging-in-Publication Data;
www.lifechangingbooks.net

13 Digit: 9781943174058
Copyright © 2015

All rights reserved, including the right to reproduce this book or portions thereof in any form whatsoever.

Life Changing Books
www.lifechangingbooks.net

Follow us:
Twitter: www.twitter.com/lcbooks
Facebook: Life Changing Books/lcbooks
Instagram: Lcbooks
Pinterest: Life Changing Books

Also follow the author:
Twitter: www.twitter.com/carlb1000
Facebook: Carlton Maurice Brown
Instagram: Carlbdreamkings

Dedication

This book is dedicated to anyone at the bottom with a vision of changing their situation to one of success. Never let anyone tell you what you can't do. The world is yours. Rumble young man rumble.

Acknowledgments

First, I'd like to thank my God for the journey of life, both good and bad. All in all, it's a win-win even when I thought I lost. The lessons alone are priceless. Secondly, I'd like to thank my family. Mom, pops, sis, without y'all I wouldn't be where I am now. You've always held me down and supported the positive things I've done. Although I might not have always gone down the path you wanted for me, regardless, our family is blessed and we survive.

Thanks to my true friends who I consider brothers: Steve, Andre, Shamon, I love y'all to life. We have been to hell and back and we still here. Peace Gods. To my Dream Kings Family...Jay, 2p's, Zee, I love y'all and we carved a brand out of nothing to make a name for ourselves. Time to take it to the next level.

Thanks to a very special young lady who inspired me to craft this story. I'm happy you're happy. The world is yours.

Peace to my guy Shannon Holmes for making me re-write this book and make it more exciting and picture perfect. I hope this book is a classic right up there with B-more careful. Peace to the struggle.

We really can do whatever we put our minds to. Creativity fuels the future. Never be afraid to be outside the box. Dare to be different. Peace to my editor Tina Nance for all the great words of wisdom and a very special thanks to LCB Books for rocking with me. This journey is amazing.

Last but not least, I want to thank the crooked-ass, so-called justice system of the state of California. Thank you for taking advantage of a young black child and clueless black family. Thank you for giving me all the time you did and thank you for making me hate you so much that I'd never give you a chance at my life again. Simply put...picture me rolling. Bay Area stand up. We did it again...

Chapter 1

"Italy! Italy! Get your ass up, and get in here. You need to clean this house. I'm about to have company in an hour. Get your skinny yellow ass up!"

Italy lay in her bed listening to her mother, Beth, yell at the top of her lungs. She put a pillow over her head and started gritting her teeth, knowing her mother was expecting the junkies she ran with. It was the middle of November, and as a tradition in the household, Beth was celebrating her birthday all month long.

"Bitch, do you hear me?" Beth said, kicking open her door.

Italy sat up on the bed and studied her mother. At 42, Beth looked 10 years older. The alcohol and cocaine she abused daily was eating her alive. An ashy grey afro stood nappy and uneven on top of a tiny, slouching frame. Italy frowned as Beth scratched into the deep-rooted craters that scattered the jaw line of her face. The high burned in her eyes as she stared Italy into submission. An abyss of hate crept up her spine as Beth balanced a tall can of 2-11 in her frail hand.

"I'm not going to tell you again. Get your funky ass up."

Italy wiped the sleep from her eyes as her feet touched the cold tile that covered the floor.

"Mom, why do I have to clean up? That's your mess from

last night. The same people that were here last night will be here today. Make them clean it up."

Beth took the last swallow of her beer then slowly strutted with a slight limp to the middle of the room where Italy stood. She stretched her arms to the low ceiling. The craters in her dark face seemed to deepen as she looked Italy up and down.

"Are you grown yet?"

Italy rolled her eyes and shook her head.

With lightening quick speed, Beth slapped Italy hard across the face, leaving the imprint of her hand and stinging her light skin.

"Then don't ask me any fucking questions. Just get in there and do what you're told, before I put your ass out!"

Italy held her face as she watched Beth storm out of the room. She slowly sat down on the flat box spring mattress that was her bed, as hot tears began to pour down her face. Fed up and tired were understatements regarding how Italy felt about her living conditions. Believing herself to be more beautiful than the drama she faced, it became a constant headache to live in strife.

Still feeling the sting from Beth's fury, Italy grabbed a mirror that sat on top of her dilapidated dresser. She dabbed her red puffy eyes with a dry towel that lay next to the mirror and stared at the sadness that looked back at her. One hundred depressing thoughts flooded her mind as she searched through her work jeans for the sack of weed she had purchased the night before. Italy steadily rolled a joint, breaking down her thoughts along with the buds of weed. She sighed before heading to the bathroom to start her day. At eighteen, Italy was even more confused about life than the first day she had her period.

As the shower started, Italy closed the door and looked around the small room. Although it was clean, it wasn't her style. Italy imagined herself in a penthouse bathroom with his and her sinks and a Jacuzzi bathtub filled with rose petals and bubbles. She could almost hear the soft jazz playing and incense burning as she now sat on the cold, white toilet smoking the joint. Pull after pull, Italy drifted into a different, deeper fantasy. A smile flashed across her face as she put the joint out and promised herself that she would make her dreams a reality.

Italy took off her robe and stepped into the hot water, embracing the feeling of a warm massage as the water caressed her body. Darkish brown nipples stood erect on top of heavy 36C breasts as the water ran over her face, further shocking her awake. As the water caressed her skin making her feel more relaxed and soothed, she closed her eyes and drifted off to thoughts of her life now and where she wanted to be.

After bouncing around from one apartment to the next, Beth and Italy had settled on Tyrell Avenue for the time being. Upon entry to the two way street, one wouldn't expect the hood that lay just a few yards away. Glad Tidings church was to the left, and white picket fences lined single story homes to the right. It was said that the city put them there to put a pretty face on the poverty that was to come.

One block away, the madness begins. Garbage and old furniture lined each side of the street in front of low-level city housing apartments. Dope fiends of all races could be seen running in and out of the buildings as groups of young hustlers positioned themselves at the first, middle, and end of the half-mile long street. Police cars made their presence felt as the "jump out boys," undercover narcotics officers, posted in the shadows of the neighboring streets, ready to snatch up the d-boys in an attempt to clear the streets for the neighborhood kids headed to Shepard and Tyrell elementary schools.

Her surroundings added to the confusion in Italy's mind, and would soon produce the black girl lost she would come to know so well.

As the water ran over Italy's head, her thoughts drifted to the abandonment she felt by every man she was supposed to love. Starting with her father, who left her and her mother when she was three, and down to her longtime boyfriend Kamal, who had moved to Florida, leaving her feeling more alone than she had ever felt in her life.

Standing in front of a floor length mirror, Italy admired her body as she dried off.

"I know I'm a dime," she said and tossed the towel on the floor.

At 5'7" 115 lbs., the weight of Italy's body was divided mostly between her breasts and butt, leaving a slim, sculpted, waistline most women would pay all of their money for. With thick, full lips and sandy blonde shoulder length hair, a man's head would immediately turn and gawk at her curvaceous bowlegs and model like walk that was perfected before becoming of age.

Italy took her time, making sure that the scent of her body was alluring before putting on a pair of Nike sweatpants and a tight fitting t-shirt.

She grabbed a plastic trash bag and began loading all the scattered beer bottles and cans that littered the small living room. A torn leather couch with flat seat cushions sat against a plain white wall, with a single picture of black Jesus in the middle. Faded dust lines from cocaine were stretched across a cracked, dusty, coffee table standing on a tattered china rug. Italy peered through the plain grey curtains that blocked any sunlight from entering the semi dark room.

Beth sat on the couch, laughing into the phone as she smoked a GPC. Italy continued cleaning as she cut her eyes at her mother. Beth scratched her head constantly as she talked. Feeling the rush of hate boil through her blood, Italy hurried to complete her task. After putting the loaded trash bag outside, she rushed to her room to finish dressing. Voices from the living room could be heard as she tied her shoes and grabbed her AC Transit bus pass from her dresser, and headed for Tanya's house.

Italy stopped as she re-entered the living room. Four of Beth's friends sat on the couch, emptying rocks onto the coffee table. Beth stood above them, watching as the need for the drug flowed from her pores. Italy pulled her hood over her head and quickly moved to the door. All four males swarmed like hungry vultures over their product. With old, faded, rags for clothes, two of them licked their ashy lips, anticipating the high they would feel.

Ricky, the cleanest of the four, glued his eyes to Italy's waist and breasts. Italy made eye contact with him as Beth paid her no attention.

As she brushed by, Ricky saw his chance to slap her on the butt.

"Girl, when you gone let me get some of that? You know you looking good."

Italy turned around so fast that she almost lost her balance. She unloaded a barrage of slaps to his face that no one expected. Ricky laughed as he covered his face and head with his arms.

"Don't you ever touch me again, you filthy muthafucka!" she screamed, turning to face Beth eye to eye.

Beth stared through to her soul, making her swallow the rest of her words.

Italy stared back in disgust as Ricky continued laughing. Quickly, she turned and slapped him once more across the face. The laughing stopped as Italy stood over him.

"Laugh now, nigga! I dare you!"

Ricky struggled to lift his heavy frame off the couch, but was pushed back into the seat by Italy. Raising her hand once more to slap him, Italy felt her mother grab her arm.

The hunger for a fix raced through Beth's stomach, and Italy was slowing the process.

"Bitch, I know you don't think you're tough? Get your

fui.ky ass out of here before I beat you black,"
she said, yanking Italy back.

The silence permeated the air in the room. Italy locked eyes with Beth as she caught her balance. Ricky broke the silence with a slight giggle before Italy rushed out the door, as the rest of the junkies joined with Ricky in laughter.

Beth bent down to the coffee table and sorted out the piece she would smoke first. She paid attention to no one; she was engrossed in her own world. The only thing she cared about and Italy knew it.

It was 2005 and the "Hyphy Movement" was in full swing. Hayward, a small city 15 minutes from the slums of east Oakland, was a relatively quiet, working class town. Nicknamed the "Stack," all the players in the game often migrated there to get away from the drama or other conflicts they faced in the neighboring Bay area cities. Often, the conflicts would follow, and leave a stain on the otherwise in between community.

Drug trafficking areas began popping up around the 10-mile long city in the mid-90s. As crack ripped apart Oakland and San Francisco, those who could escape, brought the hustle to Hayward and other small cities throughout the Bay area. Among the areas in Hayward that became street cash cows, was Tyrell Avenue. It was populated mostly by section eight housed occupants who moved there because of over population in other cities. Crack and other drugs came along with them, turning lower class youths into thousandaires.

Jason leaned back in the seat of his girlfriend's scrapper. Local Bay area legend E40's "In a Major Way" album thumped low over the speakers as he rolled a blunt, continuously bobbing his head. Always watching his surroundings, Jason glued his eyes on his longtime girlfriend, Sheila, as she came out of Bobby's liquor store on Amador Street. The cold brisk winds of San Francisco had blown over to the east bay, leaving a bitter chill in Hayward.

Jason smiled to himself at the sight of Sheila's baby face. After five years, Jason was still attracted to Sheila as if he had just met her. Becoming aroused as he stared at her large assets, Jason got back into the music to side step his lust.

Considered an amazon, Sheila stood 5'10" and weighed in at 180 lbs. Jason fell in love with the God given green eyes that rested inside of her bronze skin. Sporting an old school Halle Berry style cut, Sheila applied another coat of lip-gloss to her full, pouty, lips.

"Wipe me down baby," Sheila yelled to Jason as she pretended to brush dirt off her white puff coat.

With her matching turtleneck sweater, Calvin Klein low cut jeans squeezing her curvy thick hips, and black leather Steve Madden boots, Sheila walked with sheer confidence, not even caring that the frigid weather made her nipples stand at attention.

"Baby you gotta stop drinking all this damn beer," Sheila said as she got into the car.

Jason opened the door to the 1999 wet black Buick Regal and emptied the cigar tobacco in the wind.

Sheila adjusted the heater as Jason started the car.

"You gone have a beer belly in a minute," she said as she opened one of the Heinekens and handed it to Jason. "You know when that happens, I am gone, right?"

After taking a long swallow and smacking his lips, Jason looked over to see Sheila looking at him.

"You know your ass ain't going anywhere, so stop fronting. What did I always tell you about your surroundings? If I'm always drunk during hours of getting doe, I'm leaving myself open for anything. That damn Henny gets me too off course, because I'll keep drinking it. These Heinekens and a few blunts have me there, but still focused."

Sheila rolled her eyes.

"Blah blah blah, Jason" she laughed. "You act like a damn robot or some government soldier sometimes, I swear. Baby, you can relax once in a while. You do know that, right?"

Jason put the car in reverse. He glanced over his shoulder to make sure no one was behind him before shifting to drive and heading to their next stop.

Jason pulled Sheila's car onto Cypress Avenue. Cypress Avenue was considered another hood area in Hayward. Low-level apartment complexes lined the street, shaded by trees and iron gates, attempting to keep the riff-raff out and the little peace in. This area was one of the high methamphetamine areas. Meth heads rode bikes or walked briskly up and down the street at all hours of the night, looking for the next fix of crank or crystal. Youngsters trying to make a name for themselves stood on the corners until residents called the police to chase them away.

Jason parked in front of the Cypress House apartment complex. The Cypress House was an old hotel, converted into living quarters. Cypress ferns stood tall, surrounding the block shaped compound. Jason scanned the area, noticing the block was quieter than usual.

Sheila observed Jason's nervousness and caressed his head.

"Baby, be cool. These niggaz don't want any parts of us. I know Chico better have all the money this time. I don't know why you keep that fool on the team. You give the muthafucka three ounces, and he smokes up two then does all kinds of other madness to get you your doe back. And it's never the amount you asked for. I'ma clown his ass if it's like that this time."

Jason sipped his beer and listened to Sheila complain.

"I'm not about to stop dealing with Chico, Sheila. Believe it or not, that dude saved my life one time. I owe him, really. I never trip with him because it's only like fifty each time. I'm not tripping off that when he's handing the rest to me in hundreds. I'm not going to keep telling you to respect the game. The small shit is nothing. Think about the times you've come up short."

Sheila smacked her lips as she turned the heater off.

"That's because I used it to buy you something. Don't start tripping, Jay."

Jason lit the blunt and inhaled it deep. "What time is it?" he asked, putting his hand on her thigh. Sheila put her hand on his and moved it up her inner thighs.

"We got enough time to make it happen. Chico is always late, so you know he isn't gone be around for at least another 30 minutes."

Jason passed her the blunt as he adjusted his wide frame in the seat. At 6'3" 260 lbs., his chubby muscular frame was wide with very broad shoulders. Jet-black hair with a low cut Caesar, and razor sharp lined beard, Jason had the look of the stereotypical black male that people were afraid of. Always with a stern look, and a no smiles demeanor, Jason put fear in the hearts of local hustlers who knew him.

Never predictable, and never the conversationalist, unless it was of importance, Jason remained a mystery in the city. Covered with tattoos, he appeared to be closer to 30 than 21. Sheila's name was inked on the side of his neck.

A little light glimmered in the car across Sheila's green eyes. Jason pinched her cheeks and kissed her neck. During the five years they'd been together, they'd done everything with each other. Both of their homes were somewhat dysfunctional growing up, so the two put no one over the other. Living to please each other, Jason made sure that Sheila knew the game, and taught her everything he knew about the streets. He started her off selling weed, and six months into the game, Sheila had made quite a name for herself by not being afraid of anyone, and busting heads when needed. Jason had moved on to selling cocaine, and was seeing good money between the two. Sheila was the first and only girl he'd been with and vice versa.

Grey clouds stood on top of the stars as clear as a summer day. The temperature was freezing, but the night was crisp and welcoming. Jason checked his cell phone for the time.

"This cat is taking forever, this time. I just finished talking to him about twenty minutes ago."

Sheila looked around as he spoke.

"I don't know, Jay, this don't seem right to me. Chico ain't never had us waiting like this. We should leave and wait till the morning, when it's light outside."

Jason checked his mirrors as he let his seat up. The darkness of the street hid any danger from his view. Sheila reached under her seat for the chrome 45. Jason watched her as she checked the clip and snapped it back in, cocking the hammer back. Jason checked his side view mirror once again. His focus strained as he put on his glasses to see in the darkness.

"I don't like this. We out!"

Sheila watched behind them as Jason started the car.

"Jay, watch out!"

Sheila screamed as someone crept by the back of the driver's side.

Jason quickly looked in his side view mirror and noticed someone kneeled down by the back tire. The street lamp above provided enough light to see the outline of a chrome 38 special, and someone with a bandana over his face. Jason put the car in drive as the man stood up and pointed the gun towards the back window.

Sheila quickly held the 45 steady and let off a shot as Jason tried to screech out. The back window shattered as the man ducked quickly, and shot back with no aim. Jason hit the gas, side swiping the car parked in front of him. Sheila let off four more shots as they sped off.

Three men appeared from behind the trees and began

letting off shots at the car as it sped by. Sheila ducked in the seat as soon as she heard the first shots. Jason pushed the gas pedal as if he was trying to push it through the floor. More shots were let off as Jason watched the figures standing in the middle of the street through his rearview mirror. The men quickly dispersed when all that could be seen were the taillights from Sheila's car.

"You hit, baby?"

Jason yelled as he swerved around the corner with no regard for the light or oncoming traffic.

Sheila sat up from her seat and looked around as her frantic breathing began to subside.

"I'm ok, baby. I think I hit the first dude. I hope that muthafucka is dead right now."

The adrenaline raced through Jason as he constantly checked his mirrors to see if they were being tailed. The butterflies in his stomach calmed as they jumped on the 880 freeway, headed south.

"What the fuck was that?"

he yelled as he got into the fast lane.

"That muthafucka set me up! After all the shit I've done for that nigga, this is what it comes to? Everybody eats! Every nigga on my team eats. Ok, that's how we are getting down? No problem!"

Jason banged his hand against the steering wheel.

Sheila put the gun back under the seat.

"Calm down, baby. Let's be thankful that these punks don't know where we live. You already know we gone get them, so like you tell me all the time, be cool. Keep your head on."

Jason looked over at her as he slowed his speed.

"You're right. I gotta call Bino as soon as we get home. Put that shit back on your lap. I don't feel right at all. I know the car got bullet holes in it, so we gotta dump this with the hurry-up-ness."

"Ok. I'ma pull out all the rest of the guns as soon as we get home. Don't let this ride, Jay. We gotta get these punks back. You know this is going to spread out by midnight."

Jason shook his head as she spoke, knowing that the words were true. The last thing he wanted to do was start a war with anyone or be in any beef. For those reasons, Jason was always fair and overlooked small stuff. But now, his kindness was being tested, and he knew he couldn't let this one go.

Chapter 2

Outside of her complex, Italy watched the local fiends hustle up and down Tyrell Avenue in search of a good deal. Waste management had ignored the block for three weeks, stemming from a vicious union strike. The foul stench from garbage piled outside of each complex soaked into the pores of the neighborhood. Mexicans in big Chevy trucks drove by with their native music turned sky high, as the local hustlers rubbed their hands together on the corner pulling their oversized hoodies tight against their heads. November had come and gone, as the cold of December settled in.

Italy constantly checked the time on her cell phone as she waited for her boyfriend, June. June wasn't really her boyfriend, but for the time being, he was an escape from the boredom. Slowly, she was running her tease game on him, because there was nothing else to do. On occasion, Italy stroked and lightly kissed him, but never gave in when he pushed for the full thing. Just like a trick, June would buy Italy whatever she wanted, in hopes that she would become weak and give in to his advances. The furthest June had ever got was eating Italy out, and then begged for her sweetness as she jacked him off. June wasn't anything close to what she wanted, but Italy could not deny the gifts and the spoils of the game.

The cold bit her lips as she waited on the steps of her complex. As always, when she was waiting for June, Italy's thoughts drifted to her true love, Kamal. She wondered if he was thinking about her. Italy smiled as his facial expressions ran through her head. Feeling that warm sensation that love can bring, she quickly dialed his number and waited with anticipation to hear his voice and calm the tingling running through her stomach.

Kamal picked up on the fifth ring.

"Hello?" he said slowly.

"Hey baby! What are you doing?" Italy said, barely able to contain her excitement.

"Nothing," Kamal said sharply.

Italy rolled her eyes as the tingling died at the dryness in his tone.

"Well, I was just thinking of you and wanted to hear your voice. Do you miss me?"

Kamal was silent.

"Kamal?" she screamed into the receiver, hearing a woman's moan in the background.

"Yeah? What's up, Italy? Let me call you back in a minute. I'm kind of busy right now. My boys are over here talking shit. I'm going to call you back later on tonight, okay?"

Italy became irritated.

"Kamal, don't bother, okay. Have fun with your little chicken head,"

she screamed into the receiver and punched the end button before he could say another word. Italy clinched the phone, steaming.

"Fuck this shit, I'm getting some dick tonight," she whispered to herself.

Keak Da Sneak's "Super Hyphy" could be heard a block away. Italy knew it was June, driving his CLK Mercedes Benz. She folded her hands across her chest and leaned against the staircase, adjusting the leather coat he'd bought her and making sure her 7 For All Mankind jeans and boots were straight. June pulled to the curb, smiling, while talking on his cell phone. Italy forced a smile and got into the car. June kissed her on the cheek and continued talking on his phone as he drove off.

Italy sat thinking about what had just happened with Kamal. Quickly, she erased the thought and focused on June. His fat frame looked stuffed into the seat. June's light skin looked oily under the razor bumps covering the lower part of his pudgy face. Heavy cologne reeked over his LRG track jacket, causing Italy to begin sneezing from its strength. Italy loved June's long dreads and diamond grill, but looking at the rest of him made her not want to see him fully naked and on top of her.

"Yeah, well let me call you back in a little while. I got my bitch with me and we're about to go kick it," said June.

Italy's defenses quickly went up as he hung up the phone and put his hand on her thigh.

"What's up, baby? How you been feeling?"

Italy moved his hand from her thigh.

"Your bitch? June please. Nobody in this car is your bitch. You need to stop fronting. If that's how we're getting down, you can just drop me off back at home."

June turned down the music.

"Damn, Italy! You know how we roll. Why are you tripping?"

Italy sat silent, frowning at him.

"My bad baby, okay? Let's start this over and try to have a good night," June said, flashing his five thousand dollar smile.

Italy rolled her eyes.

"What do you have in mind, June?"

June's smile widened.

"Shit, we can catch a movie, smoke some of these good grapes, and then do whatever comes to mind. You know I'm digging your style, baby. I'm trying to make it official with you, but you acting like you ain't feeling a nigga. What's really good?"

Italy leaned back in her seat and ran her fingers through

his dreads.

"Be patient, boo. I guarantee you won't be disappointed. I'm not that type of chick, June. I have to feel a person out before I go all the way. I'm feeling you, baby, just bare with me. I have a lot going on right now. I just want to be with you tonight."

Italy leaned over and ran her tongue along the side of his ear, making June shiver and giggle.

"Let's go see Spiderman 3," she said, putting her hand between his thighs. June felt his dick harden as he hit the gas and got onto the freeway.

Spiderman was a hard movie to watch, due to June's constant harassment. Italy barely could breathe from the stench of his cologne and his heavy body pressing her into the tiny seat. Every ten minutes, Italy found herself fighting off his constant advances. If it wasn't him grabbing her thigh, it was his hand trying to dig into her jeans. Tired of fighting, Italy let him rub his hand up and down her thigh, occasionally thumping her camel toe. As soon as the last word of the movie was spoken, June grabbed her arm and led her to the door.

After the movie, June made his way a few blocks down to Chabot College and parked in the darkest end of the lot. Hesperian Blvd. was the busiest strip in Hayward. Strip malls, restaurants, fast food stops, and hospitals merged with fortune 500 companies, to create nonstop traffic from Union City to San Lorenzo. Chabot College worked as a middle meeting point for both cities.

This Friday night, the boulevard was packed with people, mostly youngsters trying to get a taste of the nightlife. The college parking lot was empty.

Italy flipped through June's CD case as he leaned back in his seat. "Damn June, you don't have any R&B?"

June turned the car off and lowered the volume on the San Quinn CD that was playing.

"Fuck all that soft shit. I like to stay hyphy, and this is

what keeps me there. Let me see that blunt, though."

Italy handed him the blunt she had rolled earlier. June paid for everything she had wanted the whole day, from the movies, to dinner and a little light shopping. Despite all that he did for her, Italy felt more and more disconnected from him. All day he talked on his phone and paid her little attention. June asked her no questions and assumed he was going to get the sex he'd been waiting for tonight. Italy felt like going home and lying in her bed, but decided to give him a chance.

"June, baby? What do you do? As a matter of fact, I don't know too much about you."

June inhaled the blunt and held it in for a moment before passing it to her. "Don't even trip, baby," he said, reclining his seat.

"I stay breaded. That's all you need to know for now. Damn it's hot in here. Let's sit on the hood."

June got out of the car and waited for her. Italy was really ready to leave now. He refused to answer any of her questions, and was rushing everything, making her that much more uncomfortable.

Reluctantly, she got out of the car and sat next to him. June put his arm around her waist and started kissing her neck. Without warning, his hand moved up to her breasts and he started pulling on her nipples hard. Italy became all the way turned off and pulled away. June pulled her back into him and continued where he left off. Sticking his hand down her pants, he became out of control.

"June! June! Stop nigga. I'm not feeling this. Take me home. You're too rough, and I'm not even ready for that with you."

June tried to continue, but Italy pushed him off her.

"Damn Italy, why you acting like a bitch? I been showed you what I'm about, and you acting funny with the pussy. Shit, bitch you owe me."

June pulled her in close to him, but Italy smacked him and

stood back. June swallowed and looked at her with hell in his eyes.

"Take me home, June,"

Italy said, starting for the car door. June grabbed her by the arm and punched her in the jaw.

Italy stumbled back as he continued to pounce on her.

"Bitch, you bold enough to hit a nigga, you bold enough to get whipped like one," he said, pushing her to the ground.

Italy's light weight was no match to June's power. He punched and kicked her as she screamed for help. Her pleas only echoed in the night as June ripped the leather jacket off her and kicked her one more time.

"Walk home, bitch. Don't ever bite the hand that feeds you."

June got into his car and screeched off as Italy staggered, trying to get up. She watched his tail lights disappear as she struggled to stay on her feet. Her jaw was numb, and blood flowed from her nose. Italy decided against calling Beth, and instead, walked to a Jack in the Box across the street.

———————

"I need you to help me handle these niggas who got at me and Sheila the other night,'"

Jason said into his Bluetooth while sitting in the Jack in the Box lobby eating a bag of curly fries drenched in ketchup. He swished the ice water around in its cup as he spoke to Gooney, his right hand man and enforcer.

"I'm not going to speak about it too much on the phone, but just know that this needs to be handled."

"Why aren't you in the house or laying low, Jay? If these fools got at you like that, you should be on the low," Gooney said.

Jason shook his head. "I'm not worried about these niggas. Getting down with Chico just let's me know they are probably some knocks or little tee-tee smoking fools trying to get some money, or some cats trying to get me out the way. Either way, no one knows my movements, and I ain't never ran from anyone, and I'm not about to. I'm more disappointed because of the principle involved. I don't want to hurt anyone, but you never bite the hand that feeds you. You understand?"

"Yeah, I dig it," Gooney said. "But there also is a thing called being smart, Jay."

Gooney had been Jason's best friend since middle school. Both of them came from poor, broken homes and always remained quiet while the rest of the kids flashed or ran their mouths. Gooney loved boxing, and had spent his time in gyms since eighth grade, sparing and learning how to defend himself. Standing a mere 5'7", Gooney had the heart of a lion. His dark skin covered a well-built body with beady eyes that instilled fear in those who knew him. A heartthrob to the ladies, Gooney was the complete opposite of Jason. After attaining street fame, Gooney became a moth to the light of fame. Flashy and charismatic, women flocked to his bold cars and fly clothes with all the pieces to match. Quick with a trigger, and even faster with his hands, Gooney feared no man and was thought to be the MAN of the two. Jason preferred it that way, opting to stay low key.

Jason picked at the fries on his tray.

"So, the word is that Chico has left the Bay, but I think that is bullshit. I think that nigga is in Frisco at his brother's house. I have a line on who the other cats were, so let's get together later on and figure it all out. Ok?"

Gooney agreed and they hung up.

Jason heard footsteps approach, and looked up in time to catch a thin light-skinned girl walking past him with a bloody nose that she was trying to hide. Their eyes met as he stared at her until she passed. A humble caring feeling crept into his stomach as he turned and watched her walk into the women's restroom. Choosing to rebel against the feeling, Jason took a sip of his water and continued eating his fries.

Five minutes later, the woman walked past him again, headed out into the cold night air. Jason watched her walk down the street with her arms folded across her chest. *Damn, it's hella cold to be out there like that*, he thought. *Oh well, there's a reason she's out there like that.*

After finishing his fries and throwing the trash away, Jason walked to his Mitsubishi Diamante, taking in the night air as the ambiance of Friday night on the boulevard engulfed him. Once again, the strange feeling caressed the pit of his stomach. Blowing out a stream of fog into the night, Jason jogged to the street side of the Jack in the Box. Surprisingly, he could still see the woman walking as cars drove by, honking their horns and making catcalls. Jason watched her continue to walk, saying nothing to the hecklers.

A car pulled up to the woman and rolled slowly as she walked. Two guys hung out of the window trying to talk to her, but she paid them no attention. "Fuck you then bitch," one of them yelled as they sped off.

Jason got in his car and drove slowly down the street. As he passed by, the tears that stained her face were illuminated by the lights of oncoming traffic. A block away, Jason parked on the street and sat on the trunk. As she approached, their eyes met again without a smile to be shared.

"Are you all right?" he asked, when she was a few feet away.

"I'm fine," she said, as she continued walking.

"You don't look fine. You're crying, with a bloody nose, walking around in fifty degree weather with a thin ass t-shirt on."

The woman stopped and looked at him. She recognized him from the restaurant. The look in his eyes was serious, but sincere. Jason watched her and waited for an answer as Italy stared in silence.

"Do you need a ride somewhere?" he asked, breaking the

silence.

Italy bit her bottom lip and nodded her head.

"You have to speak up, sis," he said, handing her a napkin out of his pocket.

"Yes," she said and wiped her nose. "I live off of Tennyson, if you don't mind."

Jason walked to the driver's side of the car. "That's cool. I'm headed that way, anyway. Get in."

Italy got into the car as Jason turned on the heater.

"I know you are cold. What's your name?"

"Italy," she said, as he pulled into traffic.

"That's cool. I'm Jason. You feel like telling me why you're out here on a Friday night walking around beat up? Females do this to you?"

Italy looked at him as he drove. His words were soft and friendly, but his face was stone. She thought he was handsome, plus, she always had a thing for dark skinned men.

Italy's voice was somber.

"A stupid ass nigga I kicked it with didn't get any pussy, so he got mad and kicked my ass. I should call the police, but I don't know his whole name or anything. It's all good, though. I'm just glad I'm still alive and that situation is all over. He lost one."

Jason stopped at a red light and put in his Miles Davis "Amandla" CD. His mind calmed and he exhaled as Miles' trumpet thundered through the speakers.

Italy watched him relax, wondering what she was listening to.

"All you can do is be strong right now. Most women would be distraught. Like you said, he lost one. Some niggas just don't know when they got something."

Italy unknowingly put her guard up and sank low into the seat.

"You don't know the half," she said in a whisper.

Jason caught the hint.

"You don't have to speak on it. We're on Tennyson now. Tell me where to turn."

Italy felt a strong connection to him, and honestly wanted to stay and talk more. Seeing Jason actually listen made it seem as if he really cared, but the fact that he didn't smile once made her think he really didn't want to be bothered and was just being nice. This attracted Italy to Jason even more.

"Pull next to that church on your right. Right there on Tyrell. You can let me out there."

Jason turned his music down as he pulled in front of Glad Tidings. Italy stared at him intently. Jason glanced at her with his piercing brown eyes. His eyebrows arched as he extended his hand towards her.

"Watch the niggas you kick it with. People are crazier these days, and not everyone cares about the way you feel. Keep smiling through it all, though. That's the easiest thing you can do in this world, smile."

Italy shook his hand. "Thank you Jason. Stay sweet."

Jason smiled at her, causing Italy to freeze in her seat. His smile was beautiful.

Italy stared at his dimples as she got out of the car. "Goodnight."

Jason put up a peace sign and pulled away from the curb.

Italy stood and watched him drive away, shocked that he didn't ask for her number or make a move on her. She smiled to herself while folding her arms over her chest and walked to her apartment.

Chapter 3

The city of Emeryville was busy as usual. Located between the hippie praised Mecca of Berkeley and the rough and tumble sections of north and west Oakland, Emeryville served as a shopping and business haven. Two freeway exits long, Powell Street square and the numerous hotels and restaurants that rested on the shores of the cold Bay area waters were the biggest attractions.

Jason and Sheila waited at the very popular Denny's next to the overpass of the 880 freeway for their friend, godfather, and connection, Bino. This Denny's was a meeting spot for many drug deals. An equal destination from the east, west, south and northern bay points, many hustlers loved the fast get away routes of the north and southbound ramps of the 880 freeway, only yards away.

Bored, Sheila continuously shook her leg as Jason read the day's copy of the Oakland tribune. Jason tried to remain focused as Sheila did anything she could to get his attention.

"What are you reading about?" she asked, pouring sugar into her tea.

"The 99th murder in Oakland. Did you read the book I gave you?"

Sheila bit into her crumb cake, nodding her head.

"It was deep."

"What was deep about it?" Jason said, flipping a page.

Seeing there was nothing else that piqued his interest, Jason put the paper down and gave Sheila all of his attention.

Sheila loved Jason, but sometimes she found herself afraid of him. Jason was too calm, rarely raising his voice, but Sheila loved the silly comical side of him when they were alone. Though 21 was hardly a child, Sheila never really understood how someone so young could be so patient and composed. Jason didn't party much, unless it was with people he trusted, and as far as she knew, that was only herself, Gooney, and Bino. Knowing all of her flaws and what her many expressions meant, Sheila thought back to the first time he told her she was lying, and how he knew she was. Since then, Sheila never lied to Jason, because there was no reason to and there was no way to hide it.

Sheila blew her tea before taking a sip.

"Well, I liked how Sun Tzu broke down the methods a person should consider and use when being a leader, and how he spoke on keeping the troops fed and showing no fear, so respect would be given. I liked that. It made me understand why you never let Chico go, before the drama. Also, the part about meditation. How when meditating, the warlord should not let anything disturb him. That book made me understand you a whole lot more. Jay, I never asked you this, but what made you get so into books? I think you're the only twenty-one year old I know who gets down the way you do. Why do you give me that stuff to read? I love it, but why do you do it?"

Jason flashed a closed mouth grin.

"Well, I remember my mom always telling me to get an education. It tripped me out, because here she was, hoeing like it was going out of style, but I always thought it had to be a reason she told me all of that. So I started picking up little books on whatever I was feeling. I wanted to know why my momma was doing what she was doing. I started reading a lot of Donald Goines books. After a while, I got burned out on them, so I started reading deeper stuff. Each book took me to a different place and gave me another piece to add to my personality. I knew I was different, because I wasn't into things the normal fourteen year old was into. I used to go sit by the ocean and just write whatever I was feeling. Some would be good, some would be crazy.

"Momma used to trip out when she would read my journals. Books also taught me that school wasn't shit. It was a brainwashing center. That's why I dropped out. How can a black man pledge allegiance to something that works every day to keep him oppressed? Why do we celebrate a man's birthday who stole a country from other people? I refused to let them make me a Negro, and believe that this country should have its ass kissed every chance it got.

"I encourage you to read, because I see the anger and hurt in you, but I also see the intelligence and beauty. In order to win, you have to be able to control that anger and frustration. Take their rules, even it out with your own, and you will win. That's all these music cats are doing now. I want you to be as strong as me. Fuck that 'woe is me' attitude. That was never the black woman's nature. The black woman has always been the backbone of the community, but I feel that is being lost. Why? Because instead of teaching and building, we chose to play that battle of the sexes game and get in all the hype."

Sheila nodded her head before speaking.

"America will allow you to lose your mind and focus, but they fight against letting you grow and get stronger. That's why they always promote parties, drinking, and all the things that really don't matter, and will happen anyway. Meanwhile, they close down schools and build more prisons. I'm not trying to be a weak, submissive woman. I want our relationship to thrive and constantly reinvent itself. Do you feel me, Jason?"

Jason nodded his head. He loved how Sheila was able to keep up with his conversation, never getting lost, and explaining in full detail. Sheila wrapped her hands around his.

"So when did you really start using the *Art of War*

methods? You've been the same since we met. You've gotten deeper, but that *you* I fell in love with is still there. So when did it really kick in?"

Jason took a sip of her tea.

"When my momma died, she told me on her death bed to always think and make every move with caution. *Behold a Pale Horse* showed me that I have to be smarter than them. That sometimes, the unthinkable thought is a pair of rose-colored glasses. Instead of keeping those methods from you, I'd rather teach you, so that maybe you'd understand me."

Sheila looked at him, smiling.

"Why?"

Jason flashed his teeth at her for a long moment. His cheeks puffed up as his eyes turned soft.

"I knew I'd love you the first time I laid eyes on you. You were feeling what I was feeling. That's why when Bino introduced us, I didn't push up on you. I wanted to see if my heart was right. I knew you liked me. When we were counting that money after that first lick we pulled together, and you told me you had just lost your mother, I felt that connection and knew it'd be me and you. When you cried on the beach in my arms that night we went out, I saw your hurt and your need to be loved. I wanted the same thing. So, besides my personal development, I gave my time to loving your crazy ass. I don't need any methods for that. When it's real, it's easy."

Jason put the newspaper in his backpack and slid next to Sheila in the booth.

She ran her hand over his bald Caesar before kissing it.

"Stop trying to make me cry, man. You know how I get when you get all romantic. Oh, I bought you a new coat."

"What kind?" Jason said, sipping more of her tea.

"A cashmere Loro Piana," Sheila whispered.

Jason spit up the tea in surprise.

"Who the hell is that? Baby, please don't get me all that stuff. I'm cool in my jean fits and sweat suits. I know it raped us, too! All that unheard of shit is always expensive. How much was it all?"

"I got it for two thousand," she said, caressing his head. "Baby, let me do my thing. I like seeing you in expensive original pieces. It adds to your flare. Now you can say you're one of the first street cats with a Loro Piana."

Jason shook his head, grinning.

"Girl, you're too much. I can't say anything because I feel the same way about that jewelry I always get you."

"Exactly! I have enough jewelry and lingerie to give to the homeless. I don't know why you like all that silk and satin stuff, but I love the way you look at me when I model it for you."

Jason ran his index finger around Sheila's lips before kissing them.

"You just don't know what you do to me, still, girl."

A black Cadillac CTS pulled into the space next to Jason's Diamante. "There's Bino. You got all the money right?"

Sheila pinched his chin. "Yes, Colonel Wright."

Jason watched Bino's small frame walk quickly to the booth. Bino was 5'4" and at least one hundred and fifty pounds. His eyes were off colored; one green, one brown, with Puerto Rican features glowing underneath a freckled handsome face. In the 70s, Bino was a fierce street hustler who worked his way up through the ranks of the Puerto Rican mafia in Florida. After the Feds moved in and shut down the majority of the gang, Bino escaped to California and became a single distributor, with his henchmen often using young kids to do his dirty work. Jason and Sheila were his most trusted pupils, and he loved them both as if they were his own.

At 43, Bino had the mannerisms of an aged gangster from the 1940s. The creased Armani slacks and silk linen shirts he often wore, spoke Florida and class.

Sheila got up and gave him a hug as he stood over Jason. Both Sheila and Jason worked for Bino when they had no one or nowhere else to turn to. Bino took the two of them under his wing and gave them a life to look forward to, in return, gaining their loyalty. Sheila always made sure to give Bino a hug for helping the two of them when no one else would. After Sheila's mom was shot during a bank robbery, child protective services put her in a foster home where her foster father molested her and drove her to run away.

Sheila roamed the streets, sleeping over at different friends' homes until she ran into Bino coming out of a liquor store. In the beginning, Sheila tried to use her best assets, her body, to gain his attention, but Bino had different things in mind for the bold youngster. After constant physical rejection, Bino offered Sheila a job delivering cocaine with his big, quiet, apprentice. Sheila accepted without hesitation.

"What's up, Jay?" Bino said, sitting down and opening a menu.

"This is the quickest you've had to re-up. Business must be good."

Jason took his eyes on a trip around the room. He simply nodded his head; Bino got the message.

"Son, you're too paranoid. Sometimes you have to lighten up."

"So how's Trisha?" Sheila said while keeping her eyes on two casually dressed white men sitting two booths ahead of them.

"You know Trish," Bino said in his native accent. "Always fussing about something, but never saying anything. My baby busted open her head on the side of the coffee table, so we've just been lying back taking care of her. What's it looking like for the two of you?"

Sheila smiled and wrapped her arms around Jason.

"We're getting married in a few months."

Bino's eyes got wide.

"Is that right? Where is the wedding going to be? Trish is good at setting all that stuff up. Let me call her to get on top of it."

Jason quickly stopped him from making the call.

"It's cool, man. We've already picked a spot. We only want you and Trish there. You know you've been like a father to both of us, so Sheila wants you to give her away. We're sporting some casual silky stuff. No need for the suits and big dresses. We're keeping it simple and us. We talked to a preacher already at my mom's old church, so everything is a go. We just need you guys to be there."

Bino smiled as Sheila kissed Jason's cheek.

"I'm happy for you guys. Trish and I will be there. Are we drinking anything special?"

"Ace of Spade," Sheila said quickly. "That or good old Grey Goose. We're going to Acapulco for our honeymoon. You guys can join us if you'd like."

Bino shook his head.

"No. We have too much going on right now. You two have a good time, and just videotape everything for me. Jason, let's go take a drive, huh?"

Jason nodded as Sheila grabbed their things, left a ten-dollar tip, and headed out the door to the car. She waited for Jason to get into Bino's car before cautiously putting the chrome plated 45 on her lap, whispering a prayer softly, then following Bino's car into traffic.

Jason looked in the side view mirror to make sure Sheila was behind them. He positioned his mirror to ensure that he could also see the car behind her.

Bino noticed his nervousness.

"Jay, you've been real antsy our last few meetings. What's been going on?"

Jason kept his eyes in the mirror.

"I've just been having this real funny feeling lately. After we get these two birds off, we're done. Shelia and I are moving out to the valley. We're getting back in school and starting a family. We both know we can't do this forever. I haven't seen the inside of a jail cell, and Lord knows I don't plan to. I'd rather quit before I do. You know how fucked up things always happen when you're about to get out, so I've just really been on top of everything. The other night, I went to collect from one of my workers, and the dude tried to set us up. We barely made it out with our lives, man. I have to do something about that, I can't let that ride. After that, I'm letting Gooney take over everything. He loves this shit. I'm tired. That was like the last straw for me, man."

Bino bit the insides of his jaws, something he always did when he was upset.

"So, who was this worker?"

Jason kept his eyes on the mirrors and the surrounding cars as he spoke. "No one you have to be concerned about. Just a dude I tried to help out and feed. I got my hand bit. What do you do to your dog when he bites you?" he said as he looked over at Bino.

Bino always felt nervous whenever he made direct eye contact with Jason. Shaking it off, Bino tried to offer the best advice he could.

"You know they say being able to still breathe is the best victory of all. Don't you think you should rethink this thing before you react? You know sometimes our personal victories can take a jab at us to let us know we are still human and touchable. I'm pretty sure the guy has left town already, afraid of the wrath of Gooney. He alone is frightening. So think about that before you set out to do what you do. Do you have a buyer for this package?"

Jason took in Bino's words as he focused back on the side view mirror.

"Yeah, you know I do. I'm going to step on this bird once, and I have some people to send it to out in Omaha. I'm cool."

"Good!" Bino said. "You have much to be concerned about outside of this thing we do. You are about to be a husband, and that is the best thing for you."

Jason smiled as the words left Bino's lips.

"Sheila wants a baby. She's been reading a lot of baby books and putting pillows under her shirt to see what she'll look like, and dragging me to baby stores and everything just to look. So in order for me to be there like I should, we have to quit this work before one or both of us gets pulled away from our child. It would be the worst for Sheila to have to have the baby in prison."

Bino drove in silence as the afternoon 880 traffic headed to Oakland slowed bumper to bumper.

"Well, I have what you need. You know where it is," Bino said.

Jason pulled down the glove box and removed the back paneling. Two kilos of cocaine sat wrapped in plastic in the compartment. Jason put his baseball gloves on and put them in his backpack, replacing the kilos with twenty eight thousand dollars.

Bino exited Broadway Street and headed towards Jack London Square. The Bay area waterfront was home to shopping, food, and entertainment. With famed eateries such as Yoshie's jazz and Japanese food, Everette and Jones bbq and, Kincaid's seafood castle, tourists to the Bay area flocked in numbers. Barnes and Noble brought in the young college kids, while the nightlife brought out the best of the Bay area. With clubs like Kimball's Carnival, The Oak Tree, and Tommy T's, the grown and sexy made Jack London Square even more beautiful.

Jason turned and made sure Sheila was right behind them as Bino slowed at a stop sign in front of Home of Chicken and Waffles.

"Alright Jay, I have to get back to the house. You already know to call me if you have any problems."

Bino turned to face Jason eye to eye, seriousness conquering his tone. "Jason, take care of my baby. You know I love Sheila like a daughter, so I'm telling you to take care of her. She's still fragile, but she loves the hell out of you.

Congratulations on the marriage thing. You two were meant for each other. It's a good thing that this is your last run. Now you can focus on living a little. I'm 43, and I still haven't lived the way I really want to. So, have fun and enjoy being in love. And you and Gooney avoid that thing as much as possible. Be thankful that you are still alive. These times are not like mine. It's hard to get away with murder."

Jason gave him a pound and smiled at him before getting out of the car. "You know I could never do my baby wrong. Thanks for caring, though." Jason shut the door and got into his car.

"Is everything cool?" Sheila asked, pulling off in the opposite direction.

Jason put up a peace sign as they passed Bino. He looked deeply at Sheila as she checked all the mirrors, looking for familiar cars.

She noticed Jason staring at her. 112's song, "Cupid" smoothly stroked the speakers as Jason leaned over and began kissing her neck.

"Damn baby! I hope we always stay getting money. It makes you horny," Sheila said, giggling.

"Let me get us home, Jay, and you can have all you want."

Jason kissed her dimples as she smiled.

"Naw, drive to Terry's house so we can pack this stuff up. Fina will be ready to leave tomorrow, so we have to get this ready for her. The sooner, the better."

Fina, Sheila's best friend delivered any and all cocaine for Jason wherever it needed to go. Being Sheila's best friend since the 7th grade, Fina did anything that was needed for the two of them. In return, Jason made sure that she and her four-year-old daughter, Angel, wanted for nothing.

Sheila nodded and put her hand on his erection, letting her fingers creep inside his Ed Hardy jeans.

"Will this work for right now?" She said, as she began stroking him.

Jason let out a loud moan of pleasure.
"Pull over and let me drive," he said, smiling devilishly.

Chapter 4

"So what club is popping tonight? We have to go somewhere cool. I'm tired of hanging around broke niggas. I'm way too fly to be sipping some lame ass drink with a foul breath, lying ass nigga."

Italy quietly sat on Tanya's bed, listening to her rant. Blocking out every word from her friend, Italy thought about saving enough money to move away from home.

Tanya fiddled with her braids as she noticed the silence in the room. "Girl, what's on your mind? You haven't said much of anything since you got here. You ain't feeling me or something?"

Italy snapped back to reality.

"Yeah, I'm listening, but I have some other things on my mind. I want to get out of my momma's house so bad. Let's get our own spot, just me and you. That way, we don't have to depend on some nigga to take care of us. We can live our lives and make our own rules. I'm sick of trying to play these cats and putting up with their bullshit. The stunt with June was like the last straw."

Tanya smirked.

"You should've gave him some and stopped being so tight with the kitty. You had him sprung. Some good pussy would've had him stuck. Shit, girl, we have to play the game or get played. All men think with their dicks, so when you give them some good, they confuse it with love. After my last ordeal with Trent, I refuse to get played again. I gave that fool my all."

Tanya modeled a pair of Ed Hardy jeans as she spoke.

Italy lay back on the plush white comforter and put her hands over her eyes. Tanya's room was equipped with all the things a young girl could ask for. She came from a wealthy family, and Italy caught herself wishing the roles were reversed. After being friends for six years, Italy had watched Tanya get anything she wanted, as she struggled to maintain her sanity.

Tanya's thick brown frame made the jeans cling to her body as tiny gold micro braids hung to the middle of her back. Smiling as she stood in front of the floor length mirror, Tanya cupped her breasts in her hand.

"Damn girl! My titties are getting bigger, huh?" she asked, holding her breasts in her hands.

Italy watched Tanya, secretly wishing she had the curves of her friend. All the ballers gravitated to Tanya's smooth, round behind and almond mocha skin, leaving Italy on the sidelines with the broke, fake jewel wearing scrubs. They'd been best friends for six years and had always had each other's back through it all.

"Let's just go out tonight and get your mind off of it all. There's gonna be some fly cats at the Oak Tree. I know the bouncer at the door. He's been wanting to take me out for hella long too," said Tanya.

Italy exhaled. "I have to work. I need the money, so I'ma go. Everybody doesn't have a happy home, Tee."

Tanya stopped modeling and quickly smacked her lips.

"What's that supposed to mean? Don't start blaming me for what's going on with you. I have my own set of problems to deal with also. I told you to ask my mom if you can stay here."

"I know girl," Italy said, lying back on Tanya's bed.

"I just can't stand this shit. I wish I had someone to just love me. Love me for me and just take me away from all this. I watch *Love Jones* all the time, and wish that it was me. I met this guy after that stuff with June went down. I felt like he saw everything that was wrong with me. It was all in his eyes. He gave me a ride home and didn't even try to get at me. Tee, he was crazy handsome too, big and chocolate. Had to be at least 6'2" or 6'3", and about 240 or 250 pounds. It wasn't fat, though. His voice was soft too. I didn't like his look though. It was too cold. It damn near scared me, but for some reason, I felt safe. Damn, Jason, why can't you just be mine?" Italy whispered.

Tanya dropped her shoes on the floor.

"Jason? Jason Wright?"

"I don't know his last name." Italy said, sitting up.

"Does he drive a silver Diamante?" Tanya asked.

"Yeah! It has 20s on it. I'm feeling him, Tee."

Tanya shook her head.

"Well, you're gonna have to feel him in another lifetime. That's crazy ass Sheila's man. He doesn't mess with anyone but her. I heard they're like each other's firsts or something like that. I know they get money and do everything together. She sells all that weed for him, and I heard he's a D-Boy. Sabra tried to get at him one time and he made her feel like shit. He's a cold dude, but hell, look at Sheila. They're good together. I don't know the whole story, but there's a reason they're like that."

"Love!" Italy cut in. "They're in love. I've seen a bunch of fine dudes get at Sheila at the club a few months ago. She didn't even take their numbers just in case. Made me wish I had a dude like that."

Tanya took her jeans off and put on a pair of sweats.

"He keeps her looking right, too. She's shining every time I see her. I caught them at the mall, shopping. They were smiling and kissing and all that mushy stuff. He has a cute smile, though."

"You ain't lying," Italy said. "I didn't think he could smile until I was about to get out of the car and he flashed those whites. I damn near lost it. He was listening to some jazz stuff. How old is he?"

"About 20 or 21. I don't know if he graduated, but not too many people noticed him. He was one of the quiet ones. I used to always see him reading or writing something. He was a little chubbier then. I guess he started working out since you said he wasn't fat. He was bummy too. He runs with Gooney's fine ass. I guess Sheila seen something the rest of us didn't."

"Those are always the ones, though." Italy said.

"The quiet cats always end up to be the bosses when they get older. They spend all their young years getting ready, instead of trying to stunt and floss. It just seems too boring to me. I think I'll get a square and keep my thugs on the side. I can't live without them. I know they ain't shit, but I love that thug passion. Jason didn't seem like a book worm to me, though."

"Well he is." Tanya said. "He still sells dope, but he is a square under all that. Gooney is the one that runs everything. Jason just… you know I don't know where that nigga fits in. He and Sheila have something big going on. Last time I seen her, she had on a real mink, girl, waist length. I don't see how she doesn't get tired of the dick. He must be off the chain in bed. They been together for hella long."

Italy thought back to Jason's smile and grinned. *Oh well,* she thought. "Let's smoke this sack real quick. I don't want to be late for work."

————————

Jersey Joes, a local Mission Boulevard cheese steak shop, was over packed as usual. Saturdays always seemed to be everyone's night to eat there. Italy moved back and forth between tables, giving and taking orders.

"Quiesha? Can you take over for me? I need to take a

break. My damn feet are killing me."

"Go ahead, girl." Quiesha said, smiling at a boy whispering in her ear.

Italy watched her flashing a fake smile as the dusty looking boy continued in her ear.

"That's why you have four kids by four different niggaz now," she said under her breath.

The night breeze hit her face like a cool massage. Mission Blvd., the longest running street in the east bay, stretching from Milpitas to downtown Oakland was busy with traffic. Italy sat down at one of the tables outside and checked her cell phone for messages. Not bothering to listen to the two messages from Kamal, she quickly erased them and listened to the others as a feeling of emptiness crept inside. Two other boys had also tried to reach her.

Donovan, her favorite, had called her four times. *He must want some pussy*, she thought. *Shit, I need some dick anyway. He made me sweat my perm out last time.* Italy dialed his number as she lit a Black & Mild cigar.

"What it do?" he asked on the third ring.

Italy smiled when she heard his voice.

"What's up, baby? I see you called me."

"Yeah, what's going down with you tonight? A nigga trying to slide through and chill with you. You wit it?"

Italy thought about the much needed feeling he would give to her.

"Yeah! It's all good. I get off at ten. Can you bring some weed?"

"Fa-sho," Donovan said, laughing.

"What's so funny?" Italy asked.

"Nothing! I'll see you in couple of hours. Make a couple of those sandwiches too."

"Okay baby. I'll see you then."

Italy hung up the phone, tingling in her sweet spot.

Italy's mind drifted to thoughts of Donovan as Tupac and

the Outlaws' "Still I Rise" album started to play softly behind her. Italy turned around to see a silver Diamante pulling into one of the parking spots. Quickly, she began straightening her clothes as she tried to look through the tinted glass windows.

She spotted Sheila's nails peeking out through the glass.

"Sheila…" Italy said to herself.

Sheila got out of the car and ran into the restaurant. Italy turned and finished smoking her cigar. Hearing footsteps behind her, Italy turned slightly to see who it was. Jason walked past her and grabbed the pay phone. Italy watched him, as his back was turned to her. Jason's shoulders were broad in his leather coat, and a pair of Evisu jeans hung low and baggy over his Gucci sneakers. Italy couldn't imagine him a bookworm.

Jason spoke into the phone receiver.

"We on our way right now. You still got the low down on that fool, right?"

Italy listened closely as Jason adjusted his glasses.

"Well, we have to make this fast and quick. I'm not trying to be long. Bee doesn't want us to do nothing. You know how a jinx works out? So let's do this fast."

Jason hung up the phone and pulled a cigarette out of his pocket. As the fire burst and he inhaled, Jason turned to meet Italy's enticing stare.

Their eyes locked.

"Hi Jason," Italy said cheerfully.

Jason stared back at her in silence.

"Do I know you?" he said, putting out his cigarette.

Italy's face became blank.

"You don't remember you gave me a ride home the other night after I got beat up?"

Jason sternly looked her over, leaving Italy paralyzed in her seat.

"Oh yeah. How have you been doing?"

Italy relaxed as his face smoothed out.

"I've been all right, I guess. I was wondering if I'd see you again."

"Well, you see me. What's on your mind? Time is money."

"Nothing," Italy said. "I just wanted to see you."

Jason's facial expression became harder.

"Have a good night, and try to stay away from these silly niggaz. You're too pretty to walk around with black eyes."

Lighting another cigarette, Jason brushed past her. Embarrassed, Italy watched as he got in the passenger side of the car. Italy couldn't believe he didn't respond to her.

Sheila came out of the restaurant with two greasy bags of food. Instantly her eyes locked with Italy's.

"What's up girl?" she said, as she opened the driver's side door and handed Jason the bags.

Sheila shut the door and walked over to where Italy sat. Jason honked the horn, waving her to come on as Sheila put up her hand to silence him.

"What it do, Sheila? I haven't seen you in a minute. I lost your phone number. Are you still selling grapes?"

Sheila gave her a hug.

"You ask too many questions. What's been up with you?"

Italy shook her head.

"Nothing, just waiting to get off of work so I can go chill with this dude. You know how we do."

Sheila laughed.

"I know how *y'all* do. I'm bout to be a married woman."

Sheila flashed her ring at Italy. She looked into Italy's eyes as she held her hand out. The envy was evident as the ring sparkled in Italy's face.

"That's cool, I'm happy for you. When did this happen?"

Sheila smiled as Italy looked at her ring.

"It hasn't, yet. We have a few weeks. Anyway, you and Tanya come through. Here's my phone number. Lock it into your phone. You know I ain't ever gone fall off."

Italy liked the way Sheila nonchalantly slid the business

into her conversation.

"I feel you. We gone do that too. Take it easy."

Italy gave her a hug again and got up to walk into the restaurant. She cut her eyes at the car as she walked by. Jason was playing with the radio. As she stepped into the restaurant, Italy heard the car start and drive off.

———————

"So what's been on your mind?" Donovan asked as he bit into his steak sandwich.

A local D-Boy, Donovan ran south Hayward the hardest. Donovan was one of the major players serving every block and turf in the city. Cocky and flamboyant, Donovan let everyone know he was paid. Flashing money and always seen driving the flyest cars, the dick riders catered to his every want. Known for a hair trigger temper, rival dealers never tested him.

Italy watched him for months come to side shows, a Oakland tradition of youngsters getting together in their flyest cars with all the trimmings, to tear up the blocks. The main attractions outside of the women were the cars spinning donuts and leaving the blocks in smoke. Police cars normally flew to the scene, shutting everything down before it could really get started. Undercover Feds dressed in Girbauds and Jordans blended in with the crowd, eyeing the hustlers to get next to. As the hyphy movement got stronger, Donovan could be seen dancing and going dumb on top of whatever car he was driving. Italy made herself visible in his entourage at every event, patiently waiting. Donovan soon took the bait, and was now wide open on Italy's love.

Italy inhaled the blunt she was smoking as she watched him wolf down his sandwich. Desperately, she wanted to explain her feelings to him, but didn't want to express too much. Italy couldn't see herself with Donovan, but the physical feeling was good. Having a thing for dark skinned men, Donovan wasn't dark enough. Plus, he only called when he wanted some sex. Italy felt her emotions were only to be revealed to her man.

"Nothing really, baby. I've just been working so hard lately, trying to stay above it all."

Donovan smiled as he took a swallow of his Coke. "You been thinking about me?"

Italy blew out some smoke as she rolled her eyes. Donovan paid no attention and continued talking.

"You know I been thinking about you and those lips all week? I just had to make some free time to come and feel them one time. You know I'm starting to dig you, right?"

Italy smiled to herself as she hit the blunt again.

"So what are you saying, Don? You want to make it official?"

Donovan threw the rest of the sandwich out of the window and wiped his mouth.

"You know what I'm about, girl. We always have a good time, and the sex is crazy, so yeah, I'm digging you. What's good?"

Italy passed him the blunt and rubbed his thigh.

"Baby, I can't offer you anything. I'm broke. Are you sure you want me?"

Donovan sucked up every bit of her helpless role.

"Italy, I ain't tripping on all of that. We will work all that out. As long as you stay down for me, you won't want for nothing. I got you, don't trip. I just got a spot in Union City. You can come post with me. You wit it?"

Italy's mouth dropped at the offer to move in with him. This is what she'd been waiting for. Finally, she could get away.

"Yeah, Don, I'm with it baby. I feel the same way about you. Let's do it, boo."

Donovan hugged her tight and kissed her neck.

"Now show me how much you been missing me."

Italy licked her lips and smiled as she unbuckled his pants.

His dick was already hard as she took it into her mouth and listened to him exhale.

"Can you handle this every night?" she asked between sucks.

"YEEEEEESSSSSSSS," he said as he guided her head back to his dick. "Hell yeah, baby. I can't wait," he said as he held onto her head.

Chapter 5

The December rain beat against the window shield of Gooney's 745i BMW. Jason stared out of the window as Gooney drove, singing along to Dem Hood Stars' "Grown Man On." The blunt Gooney smoked made the car hot. He tried to pass the blunt to Jason, but he declined.

"What's up with you, Jay? You acting weird."

Jason let the window down as Gooney flew across the Bay Bridge. Jason breathed easier as the smoke left the car. Gooney threw the rest of the blunt out of the window and turned down the music.

"You ain't answered my question, bruh. What's on your mind?"

"Nothing," Jason said, shaking his head.

The two of them were draped head to toe in all black jeans and black hoodies. Jason pulled his hood over his head and adjusted his glasses.

"This ain't something that I really want to do, but I know it has to be done. How do you live with it?"

Gooney's beady eyes squinted as he smiled. The speed of the car increased as he exhaled, staring into the wet San Francisco night.

"I don't deal with it. It really means nothing to me. After the first one, it sort of just becomes natural. This is the game we play. We live, then we die. I ain't got no problem murking a nigga. Some of these niggas deserve it."

Jason listened in silence as Gooney explained his logic.

"You gotta think of it like this man, murder is only wrong because Mr. Charlie say it is. But at the same time they say it, they sending troops over there to Iraq to kill off everything moving. Does preservation of this crazy ass country make it right? Hell naw! But it justifies it in the name of survival. It's all business. If it ain't about money, it's all senseless. That's the American way, Jay. Take from everyone and everything to get what the fuck you need, and call it business. This is business, don't you think?"

Jason remained silent as Gooney stared at the road, awaiting an answer.

Gooney cracked another smile.

"This the first time you ever had to ride, Jay, and it's spooking the hell out of you. I was like that my first one. Remember when that nigga, Black, smacked Christian? Man, that night I was scared as hell, but that was my baby girl. It still is, but I don't do the relationship thing, you know. But I knew that nigga couldn't get away with that. Fuck beating his ass. Plus, we were just starting out, and examples had to be made. Now this is another example, because everybody knows who got at you, and that it was you. It's all business, Jay. If you can't pull the trigger, don't trip. I will handle it and not look at you any different, because I know this ain't you."

"Don't trip," Jason said as he turned the music back up.

"Everything with me is good. I just don't like it. I'm still tripping that this nigga had the nerve."

The devil flicked a match as Gooney cut his eyes at Jason, unknowingly radiating evil into the atmosphere. Jason froze as the fires burned hot between the two. Jason pulled the strings to his hood as an uneasy feeling crept into his stomach. For the first time in his life, Jason didn't trust his friend. Rochelle Wright, Jason's mother, had always told him to go with his first thought, because normally it's God talking. The evils creep in when we second-guess something.

Gooney exited the freeway on Oyster Point in South San Francisco. Known as the industrial city, south city was located on the outskirts of San Francisco. Dominated by Latinos, the small atmosphere was perfect for hiding out from anything. But just like anything else in the game, you will get touched.

Gooney slowed down the car on Magnolia Ave.

"Ok Jay, that fool's peoples live up this hill on Lewis Street."

"It's an apartment?" Jason said.

Gooney nodded his head.

"Just like everything else on this hill. I'ma park the whip down here and we gone walk up the hill. I checked out the area, and the boys don't come through here much. We gone get up the hill, do this shit and run back to the whip. Keep your gloves on and dump the burner as soon as you see a cool spot. Matter of fact, dump them in this storm drain right here," Gooney said pointing to a drain as he parked.

Jason looked around the area. Everything seemed quiet, making Jason that much more nervous.

"I don't like this, blood. It's too quiet. As soon as these people hear a gunshot, they gone come outside."

"Then you better run fast or keep your ass in the car. Either way, this is getting done tonight," Gooney said.

Jason put his gloves on and checked his.380. Choosing the smaller gun seemed like the right choice to limit the noise. Gooney did the same, checking the bullets in his 357 magnum.

Jason shook his head.

"Why did you bring that loud ass gun?"

"Make sure the nigga is dead," Gooney said, shrugging his shoulders.

Jason didn't like the way his friend was acting. Everything seemed too surreal. Jason tucked the gun in the pocket of the hoodie.

"Where is it?" Jason asked.

"Right there," Gooney said, pointing to an apartment building sitting on top of the hill.

"What's the apartment number?" Jason said, lighting a cigarette.

"19," Gooney said, doing the same.

Jason took a long drag from the cigarette, fighting with his better judgment to leave it all alone, or at least leave Gooney in the car.

Jason took one more drag from the cigarette and flicked the butt out the door. Gooney stubbed his out in the ashtray and tucked the gun in his hoodie pocket. Jason put his hand on Gooney's arm as he began to get out of the car.

"Stay here! I got this one."

"Hell naw! You gone need somebody to watch your back. Fuck that!"

Jason stared blankly at Gooney as he ranted.

"Nigga you ain't never done this shit before. Trust me, you gone need me up there. Anything could go wrong."

"Are you done?" Jason said.

"Nigga you tripping, but if that's what you want, do it then."

Jason said nothing as he got out of the car into the rain. Gooney watched him run up the hill as he lit another Newport.

This nigga trying to get some nuts, Gooney thought to himself.

"Funny," he said, laughing aloud.

Jason ran up the hill as the rain beat on his face. A 5-foot high wall lined the apartment complex with a small garden above it. Jason checked all the exit routes before walking up the stairs. A smooth calm took over him as he approached the door. Peeking through a crack in the curtains, Jason could see Chico sitting on the couch watching TV.

Jason couldn't see anyone else in the house. Checking his watch, he looked around to see if there was anyone lurking around. Seeing no one, he knocked on the door and waited a few seconds. Fright suddenly gripped him as the door opened.

"Damn, what took you so..." Chico's voice trailed off as he realized who was standing in front of him.

Chico's eyes became golf balls as Jason pushed him into the apartment. He fell over his own feet, words trapped in his throat, keeping him from doing anything except mumbling.

Jason wasted no time pulling the 380 from his pocket.

"No, no man!" Chico screamed. "Gooney put me up to it, Jay. I would never do that shit to you. He promised me your spot after he took over."

Jason stood in silence as he held the gun in front of him. Hurt squeezed his heart as his suspicions were confirmed.

Chico continued pleading his case.

"I'm fucked up, Jay! I ain't eating at all, man. I deserve to get more since I'm out here getting it for you. I'm making you rich, nigga!"

Chico's voice rose as he pleaded.

Jason put his finger up to his lips.

"Shhhhh," he said as Chico squirmed. "Gooney, huh? Keep your voice down, and explain to me what happened."

Chico swallowed hard as he tried to stand up. Jason put the gun to his head and pulled the trigger before he could say another word. Chico's body flew back. Jason shot another bullet into the same spot. He watched without emotion as Chico slammed into a bookcase with his eyes wide open.

Tucking the gun into his pocket, Jason closed the door and jumped over the railing into the garden, then down the small wall. Doors could be heard opening as he ran down the street to the beamer. Jason tossed the 380 into the storm drain as he opened the door.

Gooney started the car as Jason fought to catch his breath. As he calmly drove back to the freeway, a police car raced past them. Jason took his hoodie off, threw it out of the window, and turned the heater on.

Gooney sat smiling as Jason adjusted himself in the seat, thinking about what Chico had said. Not a single word was spoken until they were in the clear, headed towards downtown San Francisco.

"Damn, blood, I didn't think you was gonna do that shit. I thought you was gonna go up there and whip his ass or give him a pass. How do you feel?"

Jason stared through the rain stained glass, ignoring Gooney's question and riding in silence.

Gooney looked over at him as he got back on the Bay Bridge.

"I understand, my nigga. We'll talk about it later. I just want to know what he said before you pulled the trigger. Did he plead for his life?"

Jason tilted his head in Gooney's direction, the whites of his eyes flashing through the darkness. Gooney looked over at him, attempting to read his eyes.

Jason stared back with that blank expression.

"Naw, he didn't say anything. He took it like a gee. You live, then you die, right? It's all business," Jason said, letting a smile form on his face.

"Right," Gooney said, glancing over at him and knowing at that very moment, that his friend had become his worst enemy.

Chapter 6

Jason woke up in a cold sweat the next morning. Soaked silk sheets clung to his body as the moon's reflection shined across his stomach. He put his feet in the thick plush carpet with his head in his hands. The clock read 3:24 a.m. Sheila's snoring could be heard a mile away. Jason walked to the bathroom on the cold December morning, and splashed cold water on his face. Water dripped from his chin as he stared into the bottom of the sink. This was the third time in two weeks he'd woken up like this in the middle of the night.

Jason exhaled as he stared into the mirror. He noticed his young face becoming older. The wrinkles in his forehead seemed engraved, and his eyes seemed to have lost their strength.

"I need a damn vacation," he said as he splashed more water on his face.

Jason took a face towel and wiped away the water as he continued looking in the mirror. Rochelle Wright, his mother lived on through his features. Jason looked long and hard once more before turning off the bathroom light.

Sheila turned on her stomach as he entered the room. Jason stopped and rubbed his hand over her butt, pulling his middle finger up the crack until it reached the small of her back. Sheila wiggled a little as Jason kissed the back of her neck, waking her up as he caressed her head and arms.

"Baby, what're you doing up?" Sheila asked.

Jason sat on her back and massaged her neck and shoulders.

"Did you have another bad dream?"

"Yeah," Jason said, moving his hands over her back.

"What happened this time?" Sheila said, trying to roll over.

Jason sat up and let her turn over. Sheila ran her hand over his face as he kissed her palm.

"My momma was chasing me with an AK-47 and I was just crying, begging her to love me and let me help her. She just kept shooting at me. Then it stopped. I looked around for her, but couldn't find her until I turned around. Only when I turned around, it wasn't my mother. It was Chico, and he stabbed me in the stomach. I woke up then."

Sheila sat up and pulled him into her arms.

"Why is it that your mom is always killing you?"

"I don't know," Jason said, pulling back and kissing her forehead.

"I think it's her death that's killing me. We never got that chance to connect, and maybe that's the part that hurts."

Sheila yawned as she looked in his eyes.

"Every time you have a bad dream, I want you to wake me up, baby. We're going to figure it out, because I can't keep using up my good sheets on your sweaty ass."

Jason laughed as she pinched his chest.

"Naw, I want you to get your rest, baby. You already know that this is my thing. I just hate the fact that on top of everything else, I gotta see Chico's face now too. I been thinking about this thing with Gooney real tough. Savion is about to get out, and I would rather wait until then. I don't know. I would love to just move away and leave it all behind me, but I can't let it go. My best friend, who I basically made rich, just tried to have us whacked."

Sheila stared at the ceiling as she spoke.

"So how do you want to handle this? We can both go and

murk him straight up. Do you think he knows you know?"

Jason nodded his head.

"Yeah, he knows. You gotta think, that was my best friend for years. So he knows me just like I know him. This is going to be a chess match."

"It doesn't have to be, baby. We can just go handle him real quick, and that would be the end of it."

"Naw," Jason said. "Death is too easy. I want to see him lose it all, first. I know everything that he holds close, so it will be nice to watch that. Don't make enemies with your best friend, you know?"

Sheila caressed the side of Jason's face.

"However you want to do this baby, just let me know."

"You know I will," Jason said.

"Go back to sleep, baby. I'm going to make us some breakfast since I'm up. What do you want?"

Sheila smirked. "A pork chop and eggs."

Jason tickled her stomach.

"You know damn well I'm not cooking any pork. We're having omelets and hash browns. I'm going to Safeway real quick to get everything."

Sheila kissed him again and slapped him on the butt as he got up.

"I love your crazy ass, Jay."

"I know," he said as he slid on his Reebok shorts.

"Get some sleep. We have a long day ahead of us. We have to pick up Fina and Angel from the Greyhound station, and I might have another connect on this weed. We might be able to get it seven hundred dollars cheaper, so get some sleep."

Sheila rolled over and pulled the covers up to her chin as Jason walked out the door.

Jason pulled his car into the parking lot of the Hayward Bart. Sheila put her Dolce and Gabbana shades on and let the seat down. Jason ran his hand over her thick caramel thighs. Her Roc-A-Wear jeans gripped her thighs tightly as Jason sat back and appraised her. A brown waist length, leather coat hung over the cream-colored outfit. Her Timberlands were brown suede and her hair was freshly tapered around the edges.

Sheila felt his stare and smiled to herself. It made her feel good that even after all these years, Jason still looked at her like he wanted to rip all of her clothes off and take her right there.

"You're too horny, Jay."

"Who said I was horny? Maybe I just like looking at what I got. I always think of how thugged out you were when we first met."

Sheila caressed the side of his face.

"Look at us now, baby. I never thought we'd be balling and living the way we want. I'm so happy you put up with me and my bullshit at times."

Jason exhaled.

"Whew. Bullshit is what it was too. But I don't trip. This is me and you until it's over."

Jason kept his eyes on the Greyhound bus station. Winter leaves blew across the sidewalks as the regional subway, Bart, flew overhead. High school kids waited for their buses while the early morning traffic thickened. Jason started the engine as a bus pulled in front of the station.

"Is that the bus?" Sheila asked, sitting up.

"I think so," Jason said. "Wait a minute and let her stand out there for a minute. Feds could be anywhere. I've been having this funny feeling lately."

Sheila blew a bubble from her gum and stared at the bus. Fina stepped off the bus looking tired. Her thick frame looked like it had gotten bigger. She wiped her forehead and smoothed her hair back into a bun as Angel, her daughter, wiped her eyes. Fina pulled out her cell phone to call Sheila.

Sheila answered on the third ring.

"Hold it right there for a second, girl. We see you."

Jason watched Fina hang her phone up and look around.

"It's cool. Let's get her and get back to the house. We have to count that money and put it up."

Jason put the car in drive as Sheila looked around. They pulled up to the curb and let Fina and Angel into the backseat.

"Damn, I'm whooped," Fina said, shutting the door.

"Jay, next time we gotta do it the regular way. Roundtrip on the bus ain't cool."

Sheila laughed as she pulled Angel into the front seat with her.

"How're you doing, sweetie?" Sheila said, bouncing her on her lap.

Angel yawned and curled up, resting her head on Sheila's breasts.

"She's so sleepy, girl. What's going on with y'all? Jay, can we stop at Burger King or something, so I can get Angel something to eat?"

Jason flashed his cold eyes at her in the rearview mirror.

"Fina, you didn't get this child anything to eat? When was the last time you fed her?"

Fina rolled her eyes. She hated when Jason grilled her on her motherly duties. He stopped at a red light and kept his eyes on her.

"In Idaho, Jay. Damn!" said Fina.

Jason shook his head.

"Are you in a rush to get home?"

Fina nodded her head.

"Yeah, baby. I'm really tired. I know y'all want to take Angel out to eat and buy her some stuff. I'll tell you what. Drop me off, and y'all can babysit her for a little while. Matter of fact, bring her back in the morning. My square ass man will be over tonight to take care of me. So if y'all don't mind, which I know Sheila doesn't, can you do that for me?"

Jason nodded his head.

"We'll do that. Get yourself some rest. Did everything else go all right?"

"Yeah, everything went cool. Cone said you better make it next time, but everything went cool. We went to lunch, did the damn thing, and I got back on the bus. All the money is there, and he told me to let you know he got the line on some high powered thumpers in case you're interested. That fool is too funny."

Jason turned quickly and stared at her.

Fina froze in her seat.

"Jay, why are you looking at me like that?"

"What did I tell you about all that? Fina, this ain't a damn social gathering or a dating service. I do business with Cone, nothing else. No drinks, no kicking it, nothing. Get a hold of your emotions. He could've fucked you, seen how loose my operation is, and got you out of the way. We're out of towners, so listen to the things I tell you. Okay?"

Fina nodded her head without saying a word, as Jason pulled in front of her apartment complex. He passed her three thousand dollars in an envelope and carried her bag to the door. Sheila watched them as Angel's light snores echoed through the car.

Jason exhaled as they got to her door.

"Fina, I don't mean to grill you all the time, but baby, this is business. I deal with you because you are a down ass chick. But if you don't start listening to at least the most important shit I tell you, you can wind up getting you and my goddaughter hurt. We're gonna keep her today and lace her up proper. Pay these damn bills and your car note first, before you do anything else with this money. If I come back in a week and something is cut off, you will be too. Do you hear me? You are not going to put Angel through that shit. You had her, so she comes first, before everything. Okay? I'm not playing with you either. Don't test it."

Fina opened her door and kissed Jason on the cheek.

"Okay, Jay. I'm going to do what you said," she stated in a sarcastic tone.

"Call me later on tonight," Jason said, pinching her chubby dark cheeks before walking away.

Sheila braided Angel's hair as Jason counted the last of the money and put it in their floor safe.

"How much more do we need to hit our mark, Jay?" Sheila asked.

Jason didn't answer as he continued to count the last stack. Sheila waited as she watched their 52-inch TV screen showing Goapele's "Closer" video.

"We're done, baby," Jason said, covering up the floor safe with their rug.

Sheila dropped the combs and stared at him with a smile on her face. "Are you serious, Jay? We're finished?"

Jason nodded his head. He leaned over and kissed her, squashing Angel between them.

"EEEWWWW," Angel said, pushing them apart.

Jason wiggled her face in his hand.

"We're actually over what we said. We're at 230. That's more than enough. I say let's cop a house in Manteca or Tracy. That'll be better."

Sheila nodded her head.

"Boy, you're lucky this child is here. I'd be all over you. So can I stop taking these damn birth control pills?"

Jason smiled.

"Yeah, it's cool. Let's have our little warrior."

Sheila smiled ear to ear as she bounced with Angel in her arms.

"I'm about to be a mommy, boo-boo," Sheila said, kissing

the side of Angel's face.

Jason watched them and secretly couldn't wait until he was a father and he and Sheila were married. He sat back in his chair, happy that he didn't have to sell drugs anymore. A million thoughts ran through his mind, especially the patience he would need to complete his GED. Deciding to start next month after the wedding, Jason picked up his phone and called Bino.

He tried to contain his happiness as he waited for Bino to answer. "What's up, angry lady?" Jason said when Trisha picked up the phone.

"Nothing much, Jason. I'm just sitting here watching Bino play with Edgar. Where's Sheila?"

"She's right here doing our goddaughter's hair. Put Bino on the phone right quick, please. I don't mean to rush you off the phone, but this is important."

"Yeah, yeah," Trisha said, handing the phone to Bino.

"What's up, Jay?" Bino said, laughing at his son.

Jason couldn't hold it in anymore.

"We're done, Bee. We reached our mark. We're out."

Bino was silent for a minute.

"Bee, are you there?" Jason asked.

"Yeah, I'm here. I'm just really tripping right now. Y'all are really done?"

Jason's smile faded.

"Yeah, we're sticking to our script. I just wanted to call and let you know. You don't sound too happy about it, man. What's good?"

"Naw, Jason. I'm very happy for you. I'm just thinking about a few things right now. I heard some troubling things the other day concerning you and Gooney. Is what I hear about a certain fella true?"

Jason swallowed before answering. Careful with his words in case the FEDS were listening in, he spoke in code and with great strategy.

"Lunch tomorrow sounds good," Jason said, just above a whisper.

"I know I told you to avoid that, didn't I?" Bino said.

Jason remained silent.

"One day you are going to regret that. If what I heard was true, you are going to have to live with that for the rest of your life. That's what Gooney was there for."

Jason felt the fires burning in him at the mention of his old friend.

"Well, I found out some other things also, since Gooney is choosing to run his mouth to you."

Bino smiled at Jason's intelligence.

"You already know, huh?"

"Of course man! He the only one who knows. I don't talk to anyone, except Sheila. That's it."

"What did you find out?"

"Everything with my friend isn't what its cracked up to be. The cold part is I believe him."

"Are you sure about that? He could've just been running his mouth."

"Naw, I don't think so. There is more I'll say in person but I know my friend. I'm more hurt that our friendship had to come to this. But I felt it, Bee. I felt it in my heart, man."

"Well on this one, I will not argue about anything. Just be smart."

"You know I will."

"I know you will, Jason," Bino smiled. "So what are the plans now that you are done?"

"School, after we move to Manteca or Tracy. These next few months will be hectic, but we got it. Sheila wants to have the baby now, so we'll be dealing with that."

"That might not be a good idea, Jay. Finish school first. You never know. You might find something you actually like and end up having to spend more time in school, Sheila also. Take everything slowly. Go ahead and get married and get the house, but take everything else slow. You're comfortable, so you can get any bullshit job. Just try to get your education right now. When was last time you stepped foot in a school? It's been a long time, right? Trust me, you will need it as you get older and keep everything legit. Without education, you'll end up back in the very thing you're leaving. Invest some of that money also. I'll cosign on anything you need. It has to be lucrative, though. Have you thought about any of this?"

Jason became somber.

"Yeah, I have a few things in mind, but I don't really know how to get them off the ground. I have to do some networking."

"Well, you do that, and take things slow. Let Sheila find out what she wants to do besides love you and have your babies."

Jason laughed as he hung up the phone and looked at Sheila.

"Is everything all right, baby?" Sheila asked, finishing Angel's last braid.

Jason smiled and sat down next to her. He kissed her on the cheek first, and then the lips.

"Everything is cool. We gone make it through whatever, so everything is cool.

Chapter 7

Italy hurried from work through the rain to her apartment complex. She put her coat over her head and walked as fast as possible. Donovan had just called her and told her that he was on his way to pick her up so they could get her moved in. Italy couldn't hide the smile on her face. *Finally*, she thought, *someone who loves me and wants to see me happy*. The joyful feeling was crippling as Italy fumbled with her keys at the door.

As she pushed the door open, the smell of crack cocaine hit her nose hard. The smile on Italy's face quickly faded as she tried to rush to her room. Beth inhaled the smoke from her pipe as specks of sunlight crept through the blinds, flashing over beer cans and overfilled ashtrays cluttering the glass coffee table in front of her.

"Wheeeeewwww," Beth hollered as she passed the pipe to one of her male friends.

Scratching her grey afro, Beth smacked her lips.

"That's some good shit there, Buddy. Who's serving it like that?"

Beth looked up quickly and caught a glimpse of Italy rushing to her room.

Italy put her coat down and grabbed a duffle bag out of the closet. Quickly, she started loading all of her clothes into the bag, checking her watch every minute that passed. Beth walked into her room, scratching her hair. Italy looked into her wide eyes loaded with hate and a high out of this world.

"Where you think you're going?" Beth asked, approaching her slowly.

Italy ignored her and continued putting the clothes into her bag.

"Bitch, I asked you a question." Beth said, yanking her by the arm.

Italy's light frame jerked around from Beth's strength. As the high gave her power, she dug her nails into Italy's loose skin.

"I'm leaving," Italy said, shaking free from her grasp.

"I'm outta this hell hole, and getting the fuck away from your crazy ass."

Beth started laughing as she pushed Italy to the floor.

"Who's taking your ugly, weak ass in? They must don't know that your ass ain't worth the pussy that you sit on."

Italy started crying as she tried to kick Beth away from her.

Beth became enraged, and she began kicking and slapping Italy across the face.

"You ain't shit, and you ain't ever gonna be shit until you learn some damn respect."

Beth squeezed Italy's nipple and twisted until it felt as if it would come off.

Italy screamed and clawed at her face. She hit Beth with a shoe and quickly got to her feet, and then slapped Beth across the face with all of her might.

Beth stood back and caught her breath. She growled at Italy with fire in her eyes as her daughter stood in a fighter's stance with her fists balled. Beth let a smile stretch across her face.

"Hurry up and get the fuck out of my house before I kick the living shit out of you. When he gets tired of the way you suck his dick, and starts treating you like the hoe you are, don't run back here."

Italy let the tears stream from her eyes as Beth turned and

left the room. "Hurry up and get out," she heard Beth yell once more.

Italy wiped her tears and quickly loaded the rest of her clothes into the bag. She grabbed a picture of her and Tanya and closed her door. Storming to the front door, struggling with the weight of the bag, Italy stopped to see Beth putting a 20 piece of crack on her pipe. Disgust traveled between the two as their eyes locked on each other. Beth shook her head as she flicked the lighter and inhaled deeply.

Italy wiped the last tears from her eyes and walked out the door. Quickly, she called Donovan to see if he'd left yet. As the phone rang, his black Mustang pulled into the parking lot. Italy slammed the phone shut and ran to the car.

Donavan smiled as she got in and kissed him.

"Damn girl. What's all that about? You look like you been crying. Is everything cool?"

Italy looked out of the window as she pulled a joint out of her pocket. "Everything is cool. Let's go home, baby."

Italy woke up in the middle of the night, as Donavan lay on his side sound asleep. Italy stared at him and smiled at how peaceful he looked. She kissed his forehead and slid out the bed, body still tingling from the sex they'd had earlier. The last vision of Beth smoking coke suddenly enraged her. She looked in the ashtray and picked out the half blunt they'd left there earlier, and sat on the leather couch, then turned on the TV. A re-run of the media case against Kobe Bryant came on the screen. Italy watched closely, zooming in on his wife.

What would make him cheat on her? She asked herself. Niggaz ain't shit. That's all to it. I'ma keep playing this fool until the well runs dry. I ain't gotta work, either. I can get used to this."

Italy admired her body in her Victoria's Secret silk slip. She ran her hands over her thighs. *Yeah, you're gonna get me through everything.* She took another hit of the blunt as she turned the TV off.

Unable to sleep, Italy began hanging up the rest of her clothes. She turned on the hall and closet lights, then stood back and admired Donovan's clothes. Suits and other expensive coats hung with dry cleaners plastic covering them up. Jordan, Nike and Reebok boxes were stacked neatly in the bottom of the closet.

Italy noticed a patch of carpet had been cut under the last row of shoes. She never asked Donavan what he did, and suspected that he sold drugs. Staring at the patch, Italy started to leave it alone, but her curiosity overpowered her better judgment. Quickly, she moved the boxes to the side, peeled back the carpet, and removed the floorboard. Italy's eyes lit up as she stared at two kilos of cocaine, five stacks of money, and a black AR-15. Thoughts of losing everything ran through her head as she traced the outline of the gun with her finger.

Quickly, everything she could think of was dismissed with the last vision she had of Beth inhaling a hit of crack.

"As long as I'm being taken care of," she said, as she put the floorboard back and replaced the patch of carpet.

Suddenly hearing footsteps coming towards her, Italy quickly stood up and put her hands on her hips.

Donavan pulled the door back and looked at her.

"What are you doing up, baby?" he said as he appraised the closet.

Italy turned around and caressed his face.

"I couldn't sleep. I have to get used to the bed. I just decided to put the rest of my clothes up instead of sitting there looking at your fine ass, wishing you'd wake up and do me again."

Donavan smiled as he grabbed her butt. He looked down at his stash spot to see if it had been tampered with. He could see that the patch of carpet had been moved a little. *Maybe her feet hit it*, he thought. Still, he looked at her deeply.

"What's up, baby?"Italy asked. "Why are you looking at me like that?"

Donavan held her close.

"What do you know about the game?" he said, looking straight into her eyes.

Italy put a blank look on her face.

"What're you talking about, Don? What game?"

Donavan smiled and led her to the couch. Italy sat down and pretended to have never seen cocaine before or experienced anything in the streets. Donavan pulled a baggy of coke out of his pants pocket.

"What do you know about this?" he said, tossing the bag on her lap as he sat down.

Italy picked the bag up and silently rubbed the plastic with her fingers. Thoughts of her mother ran through her head a million miles an hour. All the hurt, all the loneliness, and all the tears she'd shed over what lay inside the bag. Shaking the thought, Italy snapped back and shook her head.

"Is this cocaine, Donavan?"

Donovan nodded his head as he took the bag out of her hands.

"Italy, I never told you what I do, and since I have you here with me, I have to let you know in case the Feds or police hit us."

Italy wrapped her arms around her breasts and sat back on the couch. "Okay, Donavan. I can handle whatever it is. Go ahead."

Donavan looked at her with a simple expression as he stood up.

"This is it. I'm a D-Boy. This is how I get doe."

Italy nodded her head slowly.

"Can you tell me why? Why not just get a job?"

Donovan smiled.

"I'm not the 9 to 5 type. What the fuck I look like

breaking my back to make someone else's pockets fat? Living with the thought that they can fire me at any time they want, dealing with all kinds of different attitudes for minimum wage. I don't want to go to college, but in order to make the money I do now with a job, I need a college degree. Fuck all that. This way I get to do what the fuck I want, live how I want, and always keep doe. If I have any problems, that's what that pistol is for. I get to keep my girl laced in fly shit, and the rent for this spot is paid for the next six months, no struggling, Italy. You get to sit back and lounge. So, if all this is a problem, let me know right now and we can make different arrangements."

Italy's eyes bulged at his last remark.

"Don, I ain't trippin', but what if the police do come? What do I do? Will I go to jail too?"

Donavan took her hand in his and led her to the closet.

"I'm about to explain what to do if you ever see any lights flash out of this window."

Italy stood and watched him peel the floorboard back to the stash spot. Once again, she smiled when everything was in front of her.

"Pay attention, baby. Everything I say right now is very important."

Italy nodded her head slowly and watched as he pulled one of the bricks out.

"This is a kilo of cocaine. I keep at least one of these here at all times. If the police ever come, I want you to rush right here, cut the shit open, and flush it down the toilet quickly. Don't hesitate at all. Do you understand?"

Italy nodded.

Donovan slapped her on her bare legs.

"Speak up, baby. This is serious. I ain't trying to do any time, and I need to know to the fullest that my girl knows what the fuck to do."

"I understand, Don," Italy said, grabbing the kilo out of his hands. "What about the money?"

Donovan put the kilo back and covered the stash spot back up.

"Don't worry about that. They can take that. That coke is the most important thing, okay?"

Italy kissed his lips and wrapped her arms around his neck.

"I understand, baby. What am I supposed to do about money?"

"Don't trip. Anytime you need any, just ask me. I'll get you what you need. I want you to finish school, though. If you want to go to college, let me know. I'll eventually need to invest this doe into something. So you stay focused on the business end, and let me handle the street shit. Just keep it all together emotionally and we'll be good, you dig?"

Italy nodded her head, smiled and kissed him deeply. She pulled back and ran her fingers through his braids.

"So what do we do after a long day?" Italy playfully asked.

Donavan smiled and picked her up in his thin arms.

"We just woke up, but I could get used to this, nasty girl."

Chapter 8

"So what you know about real money, lil' nigga?" Gooney said as he drove his BMW slowly down Mission Blvd.

Malikie, a local hungry youngster from Tyrell Ave. smirked at the question.

Gooney took a sip from a Hennessey bottle between his thighs.

"You think the question is funny?"

Malikie shook his head as he ran his hand over his tapered Caesar. His baggy Ed Hardy outfit hung loosely over his frail body while hazel brown eyes peered out into the cold, muggy, January day.

Gooney took another sip from the bottle and passed it to Malikie.

"So answer the question, man. What you know about this real money?"

"What is it you want to know?" Malikie said, frowning from the burn going down his throat.

Gooney talked with his shoulders.

"I'm just saying, man, I see you with your little Jordans and your little fly gear, and I hear about you through the town. So I say to myself, what do this little nigga know about real money? I see you know about that chump curb money."

Malikie cut his eyes at Gooney as he passed the bottle back to him. Gooney turned down Tyrell Ave. and parked in front of the church. Both of them watched the activity on the street.

"Look at these muthafuckas," Gooney said. "Is this what the game is all about? Every one of these fuckas out here is scrambling for something they can't catch. It's like a rat race to see who will win, but they all end up going in circles. Lost in the maze, you know? I heard you making the most money out here on this block. I hear you a rider and you will get down for yours. I like that. That shows power. These punks out here don't know nothing about that. Half of them are out here trying to be tough, looking for acceptance and shit. So once again, youngin', I ask you what do you know about this real money?"

Malikie glanced at the diamond Rolex watch Gooney put into his eyesight on purpose. Smiling to himself, Gooney knew he was hooking the youngster.

"So how old are you, man?" he asked.

"17," Malikie said, looking back at the street.

"At 17, I had more money than the law allows at one single time. At the end of the day, man, that's what it's all about. It ain't about all this fly shit or the bitches you see me running around here with. At the end of the day, it's about power and money, and they are both one and the same. With one, you have the other."

Malikie noticed how many fiends were out, and he wanted to go and get the money he was missing.

Gooney noticed his hunger.

"You ready to go eat, huh?"

"Hell yeah," Malikie said, rubbing his hands together.

"I like your style, nigga. You hungry, ready to get this shit now."

"I want to roll like you. I see you all the time and hear about how you get down out here. You on some real shit. I like that. I don't give a fuck about murking a nigga for this doe. You need it, I will do it!"

Gooney laughed as he lit a Newport.

"That's good to know, but I want you to get this money out here. I'm putting together a crew of hitters and I want you to get Donovan's niggas off this block. You know Donovan, right?"

Malikie nodded his head.

"Yeah I know him. He always comes through here telling niggas they better roll with him or they ain't gone get no money over here. Fuck that nigga."

Gooney nodded his head as he let the smoke run from his nose.

"Don't worry about him. Just make sure you get these niggas off the block. I'm going to come back here with a few bricks of raw that will take all of them niggas' clientele. You move that shit like a beast and you gone roll like me, if not better. Money and power man, that's all that matters."

Malikie grinned ear to ear as Gooney extended his hand. Malikie quickly took it in his, not able to hide the excitement.

Gooney squeezed his hand hard, and leaned in close enough to smell the mint on his breath.

"One more thing, lil' nigga. If you ever try to play me, I have no problem dumping your fucking body in the bay. You, your momma, sister, or whoever. They can all get it, fucking with me. So don't fuck up. I'll see you tomorrow around eight in the morning. Be up and ready! Meet me at the Bart station, matter of fact. There's too many eyes on this block."

Malikie nodded his head as he stared directly into Gooney's eyes, taking in every word.

"I'll be out there at 7:30. You don't be late. I'm always on time for money."

Gooney let his hand go as he lit another cigarette.

"Be easy, lil' man, you work for me now. You about to see more money than you ever seen in your life. Now get out there and go get what's left tonight."

Malikie nodded as he got out of the car. Gooney started

the car and drove slowly down the street as Malikie disappeared into the first building. Donovan's black Mustang came flying down the other side of the street, screeching to a halt when he saw Gooney's BMW. Gooney threw up a peace sign as he continued his slow pace down the street. Their eyes met for one second as Gooney laughed.

Chapter 9

Lupe Fiasco's "Hip Hop Saved My Life" played in the Diamante on the Bay area's number one radio station, KMEL. The bitter chill of the morning bit hard as Jason waited outside of Tracy State prison. A heavy, light-skinned woman laughing and playing with her son drew in his attention as he stuffed his hands in his pockets. She was obviously happy that her man was coming home. He smiled, letting the smoke out of his nose from the burning Newport. The woman's son, who couldn't be more than four years old, danced to the music coming from the car.

Jason turned it up and watched him do Soulja Boy's superman dance. The woman waved at him as Jason kept his eyes on her son. He thought about how he and Sheila's child would be, knowing he or she would be beautiful, hip and funny.

Obscured from so-called civilization, Duel Vocational Institute, otherwise known as Tracy, sat just a half mile from the I-5 freeway. Surrounded by California's finest palm trees, average eyes wouldn't know about the cesspool of violence that rested just a few feet away. Double lined fences with mounds of razor wire, trapped in the destitute. Guard towers sat at every corner of the prison. A black cloud of numbing rain seemed to pour continuously over the mood of everyone from inmates to COs, even simple employees.

Jason stared at the two flags of California and the American flag blowing overhead, posted in one huge flowerbed. Flicking his cigarette out of the window, Jason let his head fall back into the headrest. He was tired of showing up at different prisons to pick up his brother, Savion. Money orders and packages were getting tiresome, but his brother was the last piece of his immediate family still alive. Savion was in prison when their mother died, leaving Jason too hurt to talk about it. After the first time he told his brother, Jason never spoke on it again with him.

Jason and Savion had different fathers. Savion's white father was still living, with a new family in Sacramento. Savion rarely spoke to him, but when he did, it was with some of the foulest words he could gather. While Jason was in school or trying to care for his mother, Savion was either in the streets or in prison. Jason loved Savion, but knew he was too loose and wild for what he had going on. Sheila always spoke what Jason felt about his brother.

A white van pulled on the side of Jason as a group of parolees got out and ran to their wives or family members. Savion was the last to exit the van. His braids hung to his shoulders and his skin was pale from being confined to a cell for most of the day. Savion rushed his 6'0" 200lb. frame to the passenger side of the car as Jason started the engine.

"What up, bruh?" Savion said, slamming the door.

Jason held his hand up as Savion gripped it tight. They held it like that for a minute, looking each other directly in the eye. Savion's grey eyes softened as he looked into Jason's cold emotionless pupils. Savion was four years older than Jason, but acted like the younger. Jason let his hand go and pulled into traffic.

"Jay, why you look at a nigga like that? You act like you ain't happy to see me."

Jason shook his head slowly.

"It ain't that, Sav. I'm sick of coming up to all these

different pens to pick you up. You're my brother, so I'm gonna do it, but man, calm down. Can you at least try to stay out this time?"

Savion rolled his eyes and picked up Jason's CD case.

"Jay, I ain't trying to hear none of that shit. I ain't got shit. I got to get on my nickels quick. You know me. Slowing down 'cause a white muthafucka tell me I can't live the way I want to, ain't my style. Fuck all that. I'm happy you're doing cool, but you do you and let me do my thing."

Jason's foot became heavy on the gas.

"Okay, bruh. When you get hemmed up again, don't call my house talking that shit. We all have to do what we don't want to at times. I don't like sending you all the packages and money, but I do. Now, you're basically saying fuck me. Okay, Sav. Don't get it twisted. I know how to say fuck you, and you know it. What do you want to do?"

Savion laughed and took out a letter from a paper bag as Jason grinned. "Jay, listen to this. This is the last letter I got from Momma. She knew everything you and Sheila were doing, and she told me to look after you. But how can I do that when I can't even look after myself? Jay, I gotta get paid. I gotta take care of myself. Believe me, I'm sick of doing this time, but this is all I know."

"Sav, that's bullshit and you know it. Right now, I don't care about what Momma was talking. She made excuses about everything too. I got $10,000 for you. What are you going to do with it? With ten gees, you can get a spot, a bucket and a cool job. I'm not in the game anymore. Me and Sheila met our quota and we're about to move out this way and get into this legal game. I'm done, Sav. Man, this shit ain't cool anymore. I been having crazy dreams, and I can't shake this funny feeling that I've been having lately. Plus, the nigga Gooney tried to have me offed. You can do what you want to do, but if you get hemmed up again, lose my number."

"What?" Savion screamed, causing Jason to swerve as he

drove.

"What the fuck you mean Gooney tried to have you offed? That nigga tried to get you touched or are you talking about some other shit?"

"You know what I'm saying, bruh. The nigga wants my spot. I'm mad at myself for not seeing it in the first place. The plan from the gate was to get this money and stay on the under, but dude been real flamboyant lately. I mean off the hook with it."

Savion ran his hands through his braids as his anger intensified.

"I know you gone let me off this nigga. Fuck that, you ain't gotta tell me shit. Dude is dead on sight!"

Jason shook his head as he accelerated.

"Naw blood, I'ma take everything from him slowly. Death is too easy. He needs to suffer slowly. Everybody eats, dealing with me. I make sure of that, but this cat has gotten real greedy. So I'ma take everything he holds so dear to him, piece by piece. After that, you can off the nigga, I don't care. But I gotta do this my way, first."

Savion smiled as he nodded his head.

"Ok, I feel that. That's that torture shit I be liking. I like to see a nigga beg for his life and all that shit. Anyway, you say you and Sheila are done, huh?"

Jason nodded his head.

Savion stared out the window at the rows of passing mountains. Thoughts of wanting to have the same feeling of quitting the game pushed forward.

"Jay, that funny feeling you're having is paranoia. It's good you have it, because most niggas don't. I'ma try to give it all I got. Those ten gees make the situation different. Jay, I got eight kids by six different bitches. I want to take care of my seeds, but shit is rough. You've been sheltered, Jay. It's rare a cat will come across a chick like Sheila. Y'all built thangs together."

"Sav, Sheila doesn't have anything to do with the way I get

down. Sheltered? Nigga please! While you were out doing stupid stuff, not thinking, I was in the wind getting doe. Listening and learning it all. Why do you think I haven't been caught? I'm in this for the money. I don't care about the women and hype. Girls get at me all the time, but I'm into a different life. The hustling was just my occupation. That's why you keep going to jail. Bruh, you got to think, *Sav.* This is a trap. They want you to act a fucking idiot. For someone who always talks about their game is tight, you always go against it."

Jason rested his thoughts as he looked his brother over.

"What did you do this time around? I see you got bigger. Was my name in anybody's mouth?"

Jason pulled a blunt out of his pocket and passed it to Savion.

"Wheeeewww nigga! Thank you! I thought you was gonna preach to me the whole time. Let me see your lighter."

Jason shook his head and passed him his Bic.

Savion inhaled deep and sank low in his seat.

"I was just working out and kicking it. I was smoking hella weed, trying to keep my mind off shit, especially when Momma died. Niggas hated real tough. I knocked a CO bitch and had her dropping weed off. Other than that, I was just waiting. Fools were coming in, telling me Sheila had Hayward sewed up with the weed. I heard you were on the under a lot. Muthafuckas don't even know what you do. All they know is that you're Sheila's man."

"That's all?" Jason asked, taking the blunt from him.

"Yeah, still be careful. Keep Sheila on her toes. You know how niggas be when they get home. She's a female too, so they'll think that's an easy lick. Every time a muthafucka talked about weed, her name was mentioned. Cats from Oakland and Frisco know about Sheila. So you gotta worry about starving cats or the police. So you're done? Is Sheila done too?"

"Yeah, she has one more pound to get off, and then that's it. It's moving pretty quickly, so we ain't tripping. Where are you living at this time?"

"Take me to Oakland. Drop me off at my baby momma's house on 92nd. I'll call and let you know when I'ma move again. I've been thinking about getting into pimpin'. Just getting a stable of chicks and putting them in the strip clubs in Frisco and on the internet. Maybe take them to LA or Vegas and get into pornos. I don't know, I think I'll try that before I pick up a sack. You ain't got any more coke?"

Jason shook his head.

"You know what? I started to save a half a thang for you, but I'm not contributing to locking you back up. I'd rather give ya funky ass some money first. I'm not going to waste my breath preaching. Get it together, Sav."

Savion giggled to himself as he inhaled the blunt.

They rode in silence for about five minutes, each pondering the other's words. Jason kept his eyes on the road, thinking about what Savion said about everyone speaking on Sheila. He knew it would eventually happen, but still Jason liked to stay low as possible. Savion took the last hit of the blunt.

"Jay, you ain't got a phone? I need to call and make sure she's home."

Jason reached in his coat pocket and handed him his Metro.

"Damn man, what kind of coat is that?" Savion rubbed his fingers against the material with a questioning look on his face.

"It's cashmere," Jason said, switching to the fast lane. "Sheila bought it for me. It's phat, huh?"

Savion dialed the number, nodding his head.

"Yeah! You look like a square, for real. You still can't see shit, huh? What're those, Gucci frames?"

"Yeah," Jason said, adjusting his glasses.

"Sheila got me in all this stuff, man. I helped create a monster in her ass. She told me to ask you if you want to come over and eat."

Savion waited for the phone to pick up, then he quickly pressed end when he heard the voice after the second ring, solidifying someone was there. "Yeah, I might just do that. Matter of fact, I will do that. Let's just make the stop first. I gotta pick something up."

Jason noticed Savion didn't let the phone ring to see if anyone was there. "Nobody was home, huh?" Jason said taking the phone back.

Savion looked at Jason with a grin on his face.

"Naw, but I know someone will be there by the time we get to town. You know someone is always home at a hood rat's house."

Jason cut his eyes at him and turned the music up.

As they arrived in Oakland, Savion got hyper and started looking around at everything, jumping up in his seat.

"Damn Jay, I missed this shit for real. Look at those bitches at the bus stop. Turn around so I can holla one time."

"Hell naw!" Jason said, continuing down East 14th, the main strip in east Oakland.

Hookers selling pussy stood on damn near every corner while their tennis shoe pimps followed them up and down the boulevard. Young hustlers and look out boys took up the rest of the blocks, causing nonstop traffic. Dope fiends and homelessness cluttered the street, causing every block to look the same. Smoke shops, liquor stores, and Mexican restaurants with taco trucks on every corner made East 14th look just like any other ghetto strip in California. With illegal traffic, also comes the presence of all police forces.

"We don't have time for that. Calm down, man. You act like you've never seen the town. The same shit that was going on when you left is still popping." Jason said.

It was like he was talking to a brick wall. Savion let his window down as they pulled up to a red light. Two dark skinned pretty girls sat in a Honda Civic next to them. The passenger sported a rainbow of colors in her braids, with a pair of gas station stunner shades. A cubic zirconia stud poked out of her cheek as she bounced around in her seat to "Thizz Dance," by the late, great, Mac Dre. A fire truck red weave lay gracefully over the smooth dark cheek of the driver. Both women, slim and eager, waved and smiled at them.

"What's up, lil' momma?" Savion yelled out of the window. "Roll your window down one time."

The driver let her window down and smiled.

"What's cracking, baby?"

Jason studied the driver, trying to see if she had a grill in her mouth or not.

"What y'all about to get into?" she asked, looking at Jason.

Jason made a disappointed facial expression as the woman smiled, revealing a bottom row of gold teeth. He sat back in his seat and waited for the light to change.

"We on our way to handle a few things, but let me get your number so we can hook up tonight. You sexy than a muthafucka, ma," said Savion, feeling like this was the first time he ever spoke to a woman.

"Thank you," she said, writing her number down. "Call me in an hour or so. Is your friend gone speak, or act like his shit don't stink?"

Jason looked over at her and pressed the button for the window to roll up. As the light turned green, he sped off, shaking his head as Savion laughed.

"Damn Jay, relax blood," said Savion. "I know you get tired of Sheila's pussy at times. Let's just click up and have a freak show one time. You know they're wit it. They was on you too, blood."

Jason turned down 92nd in silence.

Chapter 10

"Pull up right here," Savion said, reaching under the seat.

Jason stopped the car and snapped his neck at him.

"What the hell you doing, Sav? What the fuck you need a gun for? How you even know my shit was under there?"

Savion laughed as he got out of the car.

"You forget I know you, bruh. Just wait right here for a second. I'll be right back."

Jason looked around to see if anyone was on the street as Savion knocked on the door with the pistol at his side. Jason became nervous and thought about driving off, but he couldn't leave Savion there by himself. He tapped his steering wheel as the front door to the house opened. A fat, dark skinned man with a potbelly stood in shock as he stared at Savion.

Suddenly, it seemed as if the man couldn't breathe. His bald head began to glisten as Jason saw the fear on his face. Savion put the gun to his head and pushed him into the house.

Jason continued looking around through his rear view and side view mirrors as the minutes passed.

Savion pushed the gun into the fat man's forehead.

"What's up now, greasy ass nigga? You don't have much to say now, huh?"

The fat man fought for air as Savion pushed him down on the broken, dusty couch that sat alone in the living room. A sour funk came from the kitchen, making Savion's stomach turn. He grabbed an inhaler from the counter top and tossed it to the fat man as he gasped for air.

"Hurry up and suck that shit down, with ya' fat ass. You wasn't wheezing when you was on that phone talking shit. Didn't think I would make it home, huh? Who else in the house, Dale?"

Dale took hits from the inhaler like he was pulling on a blunt. Savion continued to hold the 45 up as Dale's breathing subsided.

"Ain't nobody here, Sav," he said, sounding like something was caught in his throat.

"Good," Savion said before swiftly hitting Dale with the butt of the gun, using all his might.

Sweat flew from Dale's head as he slumped over the couch. A bloody gash opened on his forehead and he felt the pain rush through his body.

Savion laughed as Dale cursed aloud, while he pulled the hammer back on the pistol.

"Ok, nigga, enough of that shit. This is the part where you show me to the safe. And nigga..." Savion shouted, holding the 45 to Dale's left eye. "I don't want to hear none of that 'I ain't got it' shit. Don't forget, I know you, nigga."

Dale was one of Savion's old stick up boys. Before Savion went back to prison on a violation for a dirty pee test, he and Dale pulled off one of the most elaborate bank robberies in the history of the Bay area. Before the money could be divided, Savion's parole officer was waiting at his apartment to take him back to prison, leaving Dale and the other two flunkies with the money, and no honor amongst thieves.

"Aight, aight," Dale said, holding his head. "Let's work this out, Sav. I got another lick right now on these gay niggas in Frisco. They got it sewed up over there on 6th street downtown. The way we get down, it'll be nothing to hit them niggas."

Savion pulled the gun from Dale's eye. After a moment of

staring down at him, Savion smiled.

"Ok, blood," Savion said, folding the gun over his chest. "Let's do it man, all is forgiven. Just give me my money and its good."

Dale smiled as Savion stood back, allowing him to get up. Nervously, he crept past Savion, hurrying to his safe and looking back with every step as Savion walked closely behind him.

Dale knelt down and fumbled with the combination. Savion put the .45 to the back of his head, causing Dale to freeze in his tracks.

"Don't play with me, nigga. You better get this thing open with the hurry-up-ness."

"Ok, ok," Dale said. "I got it!"

Savion pushed Dale to the side as the safe opened; for fear that he would pull a gun from the inside.

Dale watched Savion's face light up when he saw the money and cocaine. "So we good, right?" Dale asked between huffs of breath.

Savion smiled as he nodded his head. Suddenly, with lightning speed, Savion stood up and let off two shots. One hit Dale in the throat, and the other between his eyes. Dale's fat body flew backwards as his feet came from beneath him. Savion stood over him as he tucked the gun in his waistband, admiring the hole between Dale's eyes. A smile crept across his face as he quickly loaded everything from the safe into a duffle bag sitting on the floor.

Whose spot is this? Jason thought. "This fool got me caught up in some bullshit I don't even know about," he said to himself as he sat in the car.

As he continued checking every mirror, ducked down low in his seat, two gunshots suddenly screeched through the silence.

Quickly, Jason put the car in drive as Savion came running out the house with a duffle bag over his shoulder. Savion jumped in the car as Jason was pulling off.

"Smash, Jay! Hurry up and get on the freeway!" said Savion, ducking down in the seat.

Jason sped away, cursing as they drove down different streets until they reached the freeway. Savion opened the duffle bag as they got on the 880 south freeway ramp headed to Hayward.

"That nigga owed me 50 gees, Jay. He tried to play me and talk down on me when I called him from the pen. I'm sorry for getting you mixed up in it. I wasn't going to shoot him, but he tried to pull on me out of the safe. Fuck it though. Nobody saw us. I got a bird and $20,000. Keep your ten. I'm cool now."

Jason rode in silence, not knowing what to say. He didn't feel like wasting his breath any more than he already had. He pulled into Hayward Bart and stopped in front of the station.

"What're we doing here, Jay? What, you gotta pick somebody up?" Savion asked.

Jason continued looking ahead of him before cutting his eyes sharply at Savion.

"Take the strap and get the fuck away from me. Call me when you're safe. I ain't got no words for you right now. You put me in your bullshit and took a risk with my freedom. Get the fuck out."

Savion stared at him for a second.

"Jay, come on dog. Let's go to the house and-"

"Get the fuck out." Jason said sharply, cutting him off.

Savion smiled at Jason once more before getting out of the car.

"I'll call you later on when I'm cool," he said before shutting the door. Jason drove off in a daze. Wiping a single tear from his eye as he thought about Savion, Jason put in a Stevie Wonder CD and let the smooth vocals take him home.

Jason called Sheila as he pulled into the apartment complex before parking in the stall.

"Get dressed and come outside," he said, putting the car

in park and getting inside Sheila's Buick.

Sheila came outside in a terry cloth sweat suit and Air Force Ones. She got into the car smiling, and gave Jason a kiss.

"Baby, where's Sav? I cooked a bunch of food," she said, immediately catching Jason's vibe.

"What's wrong, Jay? Sav didn't get out?"

Jason looked at her and ran his hand over her head.

"Is everything turned off?"

"Yeah," Sheila said, confused. "Jason, baby what happened?"

"I'll explain when we hit the freeway. Roll a blunt up," Jason said, pulling out of the parking stalls, headed nowhere.

Chapter 11

Donovan laid in bed at one of his many women's apartment, smoking a Newport. The thought of Gooney passing him on his block wouldn't leave his mind. It had been three weeks, and business was getting slow. Gooney's crew was taking over, and Donovan was losing soldiers left and right. Looking over at the thick chocolate woman lying next to him, thoughts of sending her to set Gooney up materialized. Donovan ran his thin fingers over her voluptuous booty.

"Karin, wake up. I want to talk to you about something," he said, stubbing out the cigarette.

Karin moved slightly, adjusting her butt to his crotch.

"Baby, you fucked the shit out of me. Can I have like five minutes before we go again?"

Donovan smiled to himself at his abilities to fuck a woman into submission. He shook her awake, stood up, and peered out the window.

"I don't want any more of that, girl. I want you to do something for me. You know that nigga, Gooney, right?"

Karin sat up in the bed, her giant breasts hanging over the comforter as she wiped the sleep from her natural hazel eyes.

"Yeah, I know him, Don. I don't like him, though. He always runs around like the world is his. He messed with Ashley before and acted like he didn't know her, when she was all sprung on him. Plus it's just hella other little shit too."

Donovan nodded as he continued looking out of the window. The rain stopped, and the cold took its place as he stood in nothing but a pair of boxer briefs.

"So is that all? Are you sure you never fucked with him before? I heard a few things similar to that," he said, now looking her straight in the eyes.

Karin looked at the floor when he stared at her. Glancing up, she tried to prepare herself to tell him what he already knew.

"Why you always trying to play these little games? You already knew I fucked him before, so why you didn't just say that? Damn nigga, you always on some bullshit, Don."

Donovan moved from the window to the bed in a flash, snatched Karin by her long silky weave, and dragged her to the floor. Karin kicked and screamed as he punched her in the stomach and continued yanking her hair.

"Bitch, you always trying to hide some shit from me. Keep running your mouth like you won't get touched. I will beat the shit out of you every time. Now get yo' punk ass up and sit in the bed."

Karin stopped struggling as Donovan let her go and stood by the window again. Karin got back in the bed, wiping the tears from her eyes.

Donovan continued looking at nothing in particular out of the window as he spoke.

"I want you to set him up for me. We have a little something going on right now, and he needs to be out of the way. This little nigga, Malikie and his hard ass bunch of punks are fucking up my business. They take orders from Gooney, so I got to get him out the way, just to get shit back to normal. Gooney is a sucka for pussy and bad bitches, and baby you are a bad bitch with a bangin' pussy."

"Why should I do this for you, Don, when you just beat the shit out of me?" Karin said, pulling the covers up to her neck.

"Because you know I love yo ass, and I didn't mean that shit. You sitting here running your mouth at a time I'm stressed the fuck out, and needing your help. All you got to do is listen, and leave it at that. If you don't want to get down, just say no and I'll leave you alone."

Karin jumped at his last remark. The last thing she wanted was for Donovan to stop dealing with her. Karin had gotten used to being taken care of, having her bills paid, and not having to work, while her man was one of the most feared niggas in the city.

"Why you got to say it like that, Don? Are you saying that if I don't do this, you gone stop fucking with me?"

Donovan remained silent.

Karin exhaled as she stared at the wall, thinking about spending time again with Gooney. She secretly loved his style and the way he fucked her. Donovan turned and stared at her.

"So what's it gonna be? You want to keep this life or go back to working at Walmart?"

Karin threw a pillow at him as she smiled.

"Nigga, you know I'm going to do it. I just have to get myself used to even speaking to the nigga. You don't know how much I really don't like dude."

Donovan smiled as he slapped her on the butt.

"Don't worry," he said, pulling out a bag of cocaine and pouring a line on Karin's butt. Karin jigged her jelly as Donovan licked the other cheek before snorting the line off her.

"I ain't gone let nothing happen to you," he said, pinching his nose. "That nigga acts up in any type of way, all you have to do is call me. I want you to do it slow, though. I want to know everything about him. Where he cops from, how much money is he sitting on, and about his partner. I heard he has one, but I don't know who the fuck it is."

"You know what both of yawls problem is?" Karin said, dipping her pinky nail into the bag of powder. "Both of yawl are just alike. That's why yawl clash so much."

Donovan watched her snort two nails full of powder back to back.

"You know what baby, you might be right. But that just means that there is room for only one of us, and this was my city way before he ever came along."

Chapter 12

Italy drove the Nissan Sentra that Donovan had bought her through the busy downtown San Francisco streets. People getting off work cluttered every corner as she bobbed her head, singing along to Destiny's Child's "Survivor." Clothes bags cluttered the backseat as the music thumped over the speakers. Things with Donovan weren't what she expected, but having nowhere else to go, she accepted the things he did.

Italy tried to block her mind from replaying the sleepless nights and constant tears shed after he'd beat her. Because she had dropped out of school, work now really wasn't an option.

Donovan was barely home, and when he was, it was to instruct her to do something she didn't want to do. He made sure she had enough money to take care of herself, then disappeared for a week or two, leaving Italy to spend her time shopping and hanging with Tanya. Many times, the thought of leaving arose, but where would she go?

A light drizzle fell upon the windshield with the joy of being alive. Italy pulled into a parking garage and sat in silence. She thought about calling Beth, but what for? Dismissing the thought while getting out of the car, Italy made her way to the Hard Rock Café on Powell Street. She sidestepped the many tourists from all over the world, who flocked to the cable cars and the abundance of attractions the city by the Bay had to offer.

Italy took in the aroma from Blondie's pizza while she window shopped at the jewelry exchange, taking glances at the young flamboyant hustlers walking in and out with their new pieces. Italy stopped to give a few homeless people change from her purse as she made her way to the restaurant.

After ordering a hamburger and fries with an iced tea, Italy looked around at all the pictures on the walls. Suddenly, the thought of what she would do for the rest of her life crossed her mind. Knowing life with Donovan would soon end, Italy knew she had to get a career in order to survive. Not being good at too much, but interested in a lot, she shook the thought and pressure aside as her food arrived.

Italy looked around at all the people enjoying their food and conversations. Couples were snuggled up in booths, kissing and laughing, while the worst pain and emptiness ever felt was alive in her stomach. The scene was nostalgic, almost bringing her to tears.

Italy let her eyes scan the room once more, before finally allowing them rest on one booth. Her face lit up when she saw Jason eating alone in a corner, reading a book. Nervousness took over as she sat and stared at him, wondering what to do.

Italy grabbed her purse and plate, and walked over to the booth.

"Hi Jason!" she said, hoping he would be happy to see her.

The performance she was putting on could win an Oscar.

Jason looked up at her from under his glasses as he chewed on a chicken finger without saying a word.

Italy rolled her eyes.

"Can I sit down with you or are you going to just look at me crazy?"

Jason swallowed his food and closed his book.

"Sit down. It's a free country."

Italy smiled and sat down.

"Do you remember me?" she said, trying to cut the ice.

Jason looked at her softly without a peek of a smile.

"I can see you're still messing with silly niggas. Are you stalking me?"

Italy laughed aloud.

"No! Some people might call our always bumping heads coincidence. Others might call it meant to be. What do you think?"

Italy was nervous but hoping her confidence shone through.

"I think you're stalking me." Jason said, smiling.

Italy almost melted, wanting to pinch his chipmunk cheeks.

"Oh, you can smile, huh? I thought that mug was permanent."

Jason smiled more.

"Of course I can smile. I'm not a monster. But I'm not a goofy cat, smiling for no reason. Shit, the world is cold, baby. More pain than love. But when something comes around for me to smile about, believe me, I will."

"Well, you should do it more often. It looks good on you."

Jason let his smile fade.

"So, what are you doing with yourself, Italy? How's life treating you?"

Italy shrugged.

"I'm surviving, but things could be a lot better. Better days will come, I guess. What about you? You and Sheila get married yet?"

"In two weeks! I can't wait."

"I have never heard a man say he can't wait to get married."

"Well, if he's in crazy love, you'd hear it more. I love the hell out of Sheila. Wouldn't play her for nothing."

"So you've never been tempted to dip in anything else? Jason please! You're a male, and all males think with their dicks. You're telling me that you're not attracted to me?"

Jason sipped his soda, feeling his eyes become ice as Italy

stared at him with a smirk on her face. He didn't like her questioning his faith and appreciation of Sheila.

Italy caught his stare and suddenly regretted her questions.

"Jason, I'm sorry. I shouldn't question your love for Sheila. I'm just going through a lot of things, and all the pain seems to be coming from men. I just never met anyone so into their mate. This is a first. I used to see Sheila at a club turning down dudes left and right. At first I thought she was gay, until I heard she had a man. Can we start this conversation over?"

Jason softened his stare as Italy was engulfed in remorse.

"Italy, just because your situation is stressed, doesn't mean everyone else's is. I told you about dealing with silly cats the first time I met you. When are you chicks going to realize that no one will respect you until you respect yourself? Real recognizes real. Any person that loves themself will not allow poison into their lives. You must like pain, girl."

"It seems that way, huh? Jason, let me tell you something. I love myself like crazy. You don't know me. You don't know how my life has been or what I'm going through. So please don't shoot that self-love shit at me. I'm way past that."

"Are you?" Jason said, leaning forward.

"Why don't you stop and listen once in a while. Quit fronting. If you do as you say you do, you wouldn't have jumped on the defensive so fast. You would have agreed with me instead of getting out of character. If you're going to play the game, baby, stay in character. You're right, I don't know you, and really, I don't want to know you. You keep trying to make yourself known to me when I couldn't care less about you. You seem like a cool girl, but maybe you should stop trying to play with people and stay solid. Pick up a book or figure out what you want to do in life, because I can look at you and tell you aren't doing shit. If I'm wrong, slap me now."

Italy sat with her arms folded across her breasts. She wanted to slap the black off his face, but deep down, she knew Jason was right. His words made her want him even more.

"I thought so." Jason said, wiping his mouth.

"Now who are you dealing with that got you so upset and tripping?"

"I thought you didn't care." Italy said with a sharp expression.

"I don't, but this will pass my time until my friend arrives. So speak up now or hold it all in and get out of my booth. I can go back to reading my book."

Italy twisted her thick lips to the side.

"Are you an asshole all the time? I thought you were a cool cat. I see I read you wrong."

"You didn't read me wrong. I just can't stand when people blame everyone else for their problems. Whatever you're going through is not my fault or anyone else's. It's your fault for putting yourself through it. This is life, cutie pie. You better get some Cleopatra, Isis like strength in you or get swallowed up whole. That's why I love Sheila so much, because she fights for respect and isn't a coward. That woe is me attitude is old, and lame as hell. Love ya'self, ma."

Italy took a sip of her ice tea.

"I don't have anyone or anywhere else to go. Certain things, I'm forced to swallow, Jason. That doesn't mean I'm not strong, it just means I'm surviving. It's different for women. We have to do what we have to do to get to where we need to be. So if that means I have to accept the nigga's bullshit to keep a roof over my head and stay fed with clothes on my back, so be it. Everybody isn't built to sell coke or weed. Some of us have different hustles."

Jason pulled a book from his backpack and tossed it to her.

"This is *The Art of War*. Everything you just said, I won't dispute. You're right to a certain degree. You can turn your whole situation around without playing yourself or accepting the bullshit. Do you want to hear how? Or should I keep the answer to myself?"

"Go ahead," Italy said, really interested in what he had to say. She had never had a man lace her or give her pointers in life.

Jason took his glasses off and sat up in the booth.

"First, you have to realize that you are a woman. You have what niggas go crazy over and fight wars over right between your legs. Pussy is power. Hold out on it for a while and watch him flip. Secondly, demand things that you want. I'm not talking about this Gucci or Prada bullshit, because that's easy. Shit, I'll buy Sheila that stuff sometimes just to shut her up on a bad day. I'm talking about whatever you might feel. Emotional wants and desires. If you never speak up, he'll just keep doing what he has been doing. Try not to show too much emotion, because if he sees your feelings are too intense, it's an advantage, in his mind. Don't call him, or don't be at a certain spot when he tells you to. If none of that works, take the money he gives you to buy whatever, and stack it on the side. When you have enough to shake the spot, do so. I wouldn't say go and look for love, but let it find you.

"True love is persistent. It doesn't come quick and it doesn't happen overnight. It takes time. If you want to be respected while you wait, respect self and body. If the mind falls apart, the body goes with it. Do you understand what I'm telling you? Tampon this shit up. Keep putting it on him good if you don't feel like doing the other stuff. Just know that nothing is for certain, and nothing lasts forever, Italy. At some point in your life, it will all become a game of chess. Do you know how to play?"

Italy shook her head.

"Well, you should learn. I'd teach you, but I don't have the time."

Italy brightened up at his last remark.

"So does this mean you care a little?"

Jason looked up at her as he slid the book closer.

"Read this book with a clear head. It's a book of strategy.

I'm giving you this. In order to beat men, sometimes you have to think like a man. But, remember that love and respect for self is first."

"Jason, where did you learn all this? My girl told me you're not that much older than us, so what's up?"

Jason rolled his eyes and slammed his hand on the table, startling her. "Damn Italy, did you hear what I said? Don't trip on where I learned everything from. Just respect the game. If we should meet again, do you think I want to look at some depressed woman? I don't. That's why I keep folks away from me, because they're always putting themselves through bullshit without realizing it's them. Now take what I gave you and use it. Shit, expand on it. Hopefully, next time I see you, things will be better."

Italy grabbed her purse and the book.

"I'm going to read this, Jason. Since you're giving me some game, here's some for you. Lose the attitude. It's not needed. You don't have to talk to me like I'm a child or something. You have my attention, so I'm listening, okay. Thank you for it all and I know we'll see each other again." Italy said, leaving the money for her meal on the table.

Jason darted his eyes to the door as Bino walked in.

"Take care of yourself, Italy."

Jason got up and embraced Bino as he watched Italy walk out the door.

"Who's the chick?" Bino said, calling to the waiter.

"Some girl Sheila knows, that I seem to keep running into. It's nothing."

Bino smiled and opened the menu.

Chapter 13

Jason sat in Sheila's new scrapper in front of Glad Tidings on Tyrell Street, watching the activity as he waited for Gooney. The time had come for Jason to start working his pay back plan on Gooney for trying to take his spot.

Jason nodded his head to the Maroon 5 CD playing in the deck. The season of love was in full bloom, and Valentine's Day and Jason and Sheila's wedding was a week away. The block was crazy with traffic. Dope fiends rushed past his car, hypnotized by the hunger boiling in their stomachs for the next high. Jason ducked down in his seat as two cop cars sped by, making all the hustlers break and run through their getaway spots.

Gooney drove slowly past in a black '72 Cutlass and parked in front of Jason. Seeing the spot was hot, he instructed Gooney to follow him to Taco Bell across the street. After they parked, Gooney got out of the car and jumped in with Jason.

"What's good, my nigga? I ain't seen you in a minute. How you been holding up?"

"I been good," Jason said, smiling as they embraced. "Everything has been what it's supposed to. I just want to touch bases with you to see how business has been. You got that money from the last package back to me kind of fast, and I been hearing that it's on fire down here."

"That's what it is, bruh! Man, I got this young nigga on the team that's a beast. We got Donovan's niggas out the way. It's still beef, but you know how those go. World War 3 to me ain't nothing but a walk through the park, man."

"Yeah, I can dig it. I saw Christian the other day at school."

"School?" Gooney said, lighting a Newport.

"Yeah nigga, school. That's what I do all day now. I go to school and stay out the way. I'm loving this retirement shit."

"Enjoy yourself, then. How did she look? I miss the hell out of that girl, but I know we can't be together. She just ain't going for me. Was she still fly?"

"As always. She just getting it all together. Anyway, how has the business been? You getting fat without me here?"

"I ain't gone lie, Jay, you quitting this shit was the best thing to happen to me, but I miss you at the same time. You know how long we been together. It's like I miss a piece of me, you dig?"

Jason nodded his head as he looked into the flowing traffic.

"So what you think you're sitting on now?" Jason asked, looking over at Gooney.

Smiling, Gooney put his hands behind his head as he blew out a ring of smoke.

"I'd say around four or five. It's all tucked in the safe too, bruh. You should see the shit when I open it, Jay. I fucked the shit out of this bitch I use to fuck a while back, on top of it. Shit is getting out, man. Niggas can't fuck with me out here. I'm bout to get another condo in those new skyscrapers that they built in Frisco. You know the ones you can see from the bridge as soon as you get past Treasure Island? Those!"

Jason smiled to himself as Gooney let him know everything he wanted to know. Gooney answered his phone as Jason turned down the music.

"Jay, this the young nigga right here I was telling you

about. He about to come over and drop this money off to me."

Jason nodded as Gooney hung up the phone.

"I love this shit, Jay. You can't tell me that you don't miss it a little bit."

Jason shook his head as a dark blue Chrysler 300 pulled on the side of them.

"Look how I got this young nigga ridin'. We getting it out here, Jay."

Malikie let the window down and tossed a duffle bag into the car. Jason watched as Gooney unzipped the bag and counted the money.

"It's all there, nigga." Malikie said.

"I know that. You know better than to bite the hand that feeds you," Gooney said, zipping the bag up and putting it between his legs.

"Malikie, this my man, Jay. He the one that got this whole shit started with me back in the day. Respect this nigga like you do me when you see him. He a real factor!"

Malikie leaned forward to get a better look at Jason, and put up a peace sign as he inspected his face. Jason looked in Malikie's car and face before leaning back in his seat.

"Don't trip," Gooney said. "He don't talk much. Stay off the block for a second. The boys just went through there on some sweep shit."

"For real?" Malikie said, starting his car. "I'll be good. That nigga Donovan came through here the other day. He didn't do shit, but I'm putting niggas on alert just in case he try to send his boys."

"That nigga ain't about to do nothing. He smart enough to recognize defeat. Don't even trip."

Jason took this as a time to get respect out of Malikie.

"Don't listen to this nigga, youngster. You doing the right thing by putting niggas on alert. Donovan is smart, and that's why you put them on alert. He ain't just gone take a loss lying down, I know that dude."

"Right on, Jay. I'ma do that right now. I'll holler at y'all."

Gooney let the window up as Malikie pulled off.

Jason sat back in his seat and started the car.

Gooney shook his head as he lit another cigarette.

"What?" Jason said, noticing that going over Gooney's head had gotten under his skin.

"That wasn't cool, Jay. You made it look like I don't know what I'm doing, blood. Youngsters lose respect for niggas like that."

"I didn't mean for that to happen, but you got to be aware of a nigga like Donovan. You know that nigga, just like I do. Would you ever back down?"

"Hell naw. I'ma come at a nigga five times harder."

"And you and Donovan are one and the same," Jason said, extending his hand.

"Be careful out here, my nigga. Watch the niggas you think you know. They just might strike if you don't cut the grass."

Gooney got out of the car.

"Tell Sheila I said what's up, blood. Take care of yourself, and tell Christian I still love her next time you see her."

Jason pulled out of the parking lot, feeling better than he did when he pulled up. Everything was falling into place, as it was meant to be.

Chapter 14

"Damn it's cold out here, Jay. I'm not feeling this at all."

Two days later, Jason and Sheila stood in front of the Wienerschnitzel in Hayward on A Street. The below level temperatures, mixed with the 20 mile an hour winds, caused numb ears and runny noses.

"This fool is too paranoid. Let's go inside and wait for him. My damn nipples are about to fall off." Sheila said, bundling up her puff coat.

Jason pulled his beanie down low over his eyes as he bobbed his shoulders up and down in his pea coat. Sheila did the same. He wrapped his arms around her waist and held her close to him.

"Think this might warm you up?" he said, letting his hands fall down to her butt.

"Naw, but a hot oil massage later will do."

Jason kissed the top of her forehead before heading into the restaurant.

"Jay, I know Sav is your brother and you love him, but baby, this nigga is too hot right now. Every time he gets out, it's the same thing. Why didn't he just come to the house?"

Jason looked out of the window at all the cars passing by. The waitress came over to take their order. They ordered no food, just a coffee and hot chocolate. Savion had called him early in the morning to tell him to meet him. He said he had some important information that needed to be said in person. Jason unzipped his coat and sat back in the seat.

Sheila leaned her head on his shoulder as Jason bit his bottom lip. Sheila noticed the biting and gently pulled his lip from his teeth.

"Stop that. You know I can't stand that. What's on your mind?"

Jason exhaled and patted her head.

"Sav sounded scared. I never heard Sav sound like that. He's always cocky as hell on the phone. This time, he sounded like it was almost over, or someone was after him. I'm just wondering what kind of shit he's got himself into. Whatever it is, I gotta help him. That's the only family I have left."

"No it's not." Sheila said, caressing the side of his face. "Look baby, Sav is a grown man. You can't keep running to his aid every time something happens. I know you want to help him through everything, but he has to learn to stand on his own two feet. The fool doesn't ever listen to what you tell him, but you're the first one he calls every time something pops. Leave him alone for a minute and let him figure things out for himself."

Jason rubbed his hand up and down the length of her arm.

"I feel you, baby. I really do. But I can't. Do you know my momma spent her last hours of breath talking about Sav? Every move she made, hurt, because she was in so much pain. But she cried over Savion. She was mad at herself for the way he turned out. Believe me, I would love to let Sav fly, but I promised my momma we'd stay tight, connected, and that we would function as brothers. As family. That's all she wanted, because our relationship was so loose while she was alive. That's why I can't turn my back on Sav."

Sheila understood where Jason was coming from. Deep down, she felt that one day she'd lose Jason over Savion's madness. She always spoke her mind, but knew that she wouldn't be able to come between them. Jason and Savion were linked together by fire, and a pain unknown to any outsiders, further causing Sheila to not want any harm to be brought to Jason.

"I understand, baby," Sheila said, stretching her arms. "But just be careful of everything. I don't want to lose you to any bullshit."

They wacthed from inside as a green '97 Monte Carlo screeched into the parking lot and slammed on the brakes. Jason could see Savion's outline through the tinted glass.

"Here he comes now," Jason said, sitting up in the booth.

Savion pulled the hood of his sweatshirt over his head. He threw the cigarette he was smoking, as he rushed into the restaurant. Scanning the room until he saw Jason and Sheila, a feeling of calm took over him.

"What up, Jay?" he said, barely audible.

Jason put his hand up and waited for him to grab it. Savion held his hand with his for a few tight seconds.

"What's going on, Sav? You look like shit."

Sheila reached over and tried to pull his hood off, but he slapped her hand away.

"What the fuck you doing, Sheila?" said Savion. "I put it on for a reason, okay. What you want some attention? How are you doing? You look good and all that other shit."

Sheila frowned and smacked her lips.

"I'm trying to see your eyes. When was the last time you went to sleep, Sav?"

"I just got out of the hospital. I had to get some stitches in the back of my head." Savion took his shades off and revealed two swollen purple and black eyes.

"What the fuck happened to you?" Jason asked, leaning forward for a better look.

The side of Savion's face was swollen purple and red.

"Man, shit hit the fan hard. After you dropped me off, I

went to Frisco and was holed up in a little hotel. That fat fuck, Dale, told me about a lick before it was over. I still had that bird, and there were hella fiends running around. You know how it is on Sixth Street in the city. Anyway, I knocked this little smoker broad, and she started bringing me clientele. So, I cooked the coke up and stepped on it real good. I started serving 20s until I ran out. I bought some gear and everything, and was getting doe. Anyway, I went to the little Chinese food spot on Seventh Street real quick and came back."

Sheila and Jason listened intently as Sav continued.

"When I opened the door, I see muthafuckas leaned over the bed choking the hell out of the smoker broad. I knew it was a jack, so I started to run. I left my gun in the room, so I didn't have any protection, and these niggas had choppers. Soon as I turned around, somebody punched me in the face. I fell down and they started beating the shit out of me. They pulled me in the room and started again. One of them was talking about killing the broad, but I didn't give a fuck about her in the first place."

Sav removed his hoodie and quickly returned it to its resting place, concealing the stitches.

"They knocked her out and put a Tec in my mouth. In my fucking mouth, *Jay*. The dope isn't worth dying over, so I showed them where it was. They knocked me out along with the bitch and got everything. I woke up in the hospital with bruised ribs and all kinds of other shit. I'm taped up real good under here. I'm on the run from my parole officer, too. Did you happen to see that murder on the news after we split?"

Jason nodded his head.

"Jay, I know who the niggas are that got me at the hotel. I was in the pen with one of the faggot fucks. I know his name, and where he's from, too. I'ma get his ass and the others if I can, but I need to get on line with some heat. I'm talking real shit. Not those little hand guns you like. I need a SK or a Mac. I need someone to have my back, too. What's up, Jay? Let's serve these niggas."

Sheila quickly began shaking her head.

"No, no, no, no! See Jay, this is why I told you what I told you. Sav, why don't you just chill? You always come home on some ill shit, and expect Jason to bail you out every time. What goes around comes around. You came home out the gates, *not even two hours*, and did some crazy shit. Now it happened to you, so live with it. Jason isn't getting involved with that. I'm not having it."

Savion waved his hand at her.

"Jay, why did you bring this bitch? Sheila, I'm not trying to hear your shit. This ain't got anything to do with you. This is between me and my brother. Why don't you just shut the fuck up and play your position. I can handle my own business, but I need help this time. Jason is a grown fucking man. He can make his own decisions. Why don't you let him do that, instead of trying to think for him? Shit, he made you. So let him speak for himself."

"No you didn't call me a bitch." Sheila said, jumping up. "You broke-ass, stupid muthafucka, all you do is call on someone for help. 'Jay, I'm in the pen, Jay I need some money, Jay, Jay, Jay, Jay.' Grow up, nigga. You ain't hard, Sav. You just do shit to do it. You better watch who the fuck you're talking to before you get fucked up!"

Savion stood up and put his finger in her face.

"Sheila, you better sit the hell down and shut your fucking mouth before-"

"Both of you shut the fuck up and sit down. You want the whole city knowing your business? Act like you got some sense. Sit down!" Jason said firmly.

Both of them sat down, while Jason smiled at the manager who'd come out to see what all the commotion was about. Jason put his hand up and nodded his head before darting his eyes at Savion.

"Look, first of all, learn to control yourself. You got all

these people looking at us, and now they're ear-hustling, trying to figure out what's going on. For a man that's on the run, you sure don't act like it. Second, Sheila, let me handle this. I love you for voicing your opinion and looking out, but Sav is right. Play your position right now."

Sheila smacked her lips and looked at him coldly.

"Sav, I can't get involved in all that," said Jason. "I can get you on line with some heat, but this is your mess, you have to clean it up. I told you when I picked you up that I was tired. That I was done, I'm moving on, man. It's time to grow up. You're putting my life in jeopardy with your recklessness. I can't keep getting down like this with you, blood. I love you, and you know I do. I think that's why you always come at me with this shit. Now I still got ten thousand for you. If you still feel that you have to get at those cats, that choice is yours. But I can't get involved."

"They fucked me in my ass, Jay. Damn, do you understand now? I got stitches in my ass, Jay. It hurts to even sit down. They fucked me, Jay. They did me." Savion said calmly, staring at the table, too ashamed to look into Jason's eyes.

Leaning back in the chair, he covered his face to hide the tears.

Jason became blank as he stared at Savion in shock. Sheila's mouth hung open.

"Fuck it," Savion said, slowly getting up. "You don't want to have my back, fuck you. I'll handle the shit myself. Fuck you and this bitch."

Savion pulled the strings on his hoodie tight and put his shades back on as he headed towards the exit. Jason remained speechless as he watched Savion get into the car.

Sheila stared down at the table as Jason suddenly moved her out of the way and ran out of the restaurant.

Savion stopped the car as burning tears poured down his face while he struggled to gather himself. Jason saw the child in him as his swollen dark eyes begged for help under a wet, tear stained face.

Jason yanked the door open and wrapped Savion up in his arms. Silence was the only speaker for what seemed like an eternity.

"Never again, man! Let's get these cats. I'm sorry, Sav. I'm sorry!"

Savion let the tears flow as Jason held him in his arms.

"Drive to the house and we'll get you cleaned up and figure out our next move."

Savion nodded and wiped his face.

"I'll meet you there. Jay, I love you man. You're the only one I can call on, that's why I do."

"Don't trip," said Jason as he shut the car door.

Jason watched Savion pull into traffic before walking to his car. Sheila came out of the restaurant and walked quietly beside him.

"Call Fina and tell her I'm going to need her to do something. I can't turn my back on this one, Sheila. I can't."

Sheila pursed her lips, looking at him softly.

"Jason, I understand. I'm not going to say anything. Really, I want in on this one."

"No, this is going to be the grimiest one ever. I can't believe all this shit is happening. With everything else going on with Gooney, and just the fact that I'm trying to leave all this bullshit alone. It's killing me, Sheila."

Sheila looked off into the traffic as mist from the cold blew softly from her nose.

"Maybe we should leave all of it alone right now and just run away before success takes a good shot at you. A smart man knows when to stop, and you are smart Jay."

Jason looked up into the grey cloudy emptiness of the sky as he spoke.

"Naw, I ain't never ran from anyone, and I'm not about to start. I feel Savion's pain like it was my own, so I can't run from this one or any other one. These niggas have to pay, just like Gooney. The only difference with this one, is it has to be quick and fast. Every time a guy tries to quit, it's always something to call him right back."

Chapter 15

"Yo, let that water boil a little more. I wanna get this shit cooked up fast, so we can hit the block fast. It's the first of the month, blood, and you know they gone be out there thick."

Malikie stood at a beat up, wood chipped, kitchen table in Beth's apartment, adding baking soda to an ounce of cocaine. Beth looked on, her eyes growing bigger with every ounce that was ready. Malikie turned to see her staring at the rocks that he had bundled up on the table. A single Mac-11 lay next to the finished product as Whip, Malikie's right hand man, chopped everything down after it became cool. Carlos, the new man in the clique, bagged everything up as Malikie stood over everything, talking on his Bluetooth and keeping an eye on Beth.

Fella, the official cook of the group stood over the stove, mixing the product together.

"Damn, it's hot in this muthafucka. You ain't got a fan?" he said to Beth.

"Naw, it broke last week," Beth said as she licked her lips, never taking an eye off the rocks.

Malikie cut his eyes at her.

"You ready to try this shit, lady?"

Beth nodded eagerly as she stepped forward.

Malikie handed her three rocks out of the pile and watched her scatter to the other room.

"These muthafuckas is crazy," he said shaking his head.

"Who dat?" Carlos said.

"Knocks! You see how she just ran off like that. The bitch didn't even say thank you. I bet she smoke those up in two minutes, and be in here begging for more. The cold thing is, she ain't gone ask, she just gone stand there looking pitiful."

Malikie turned the Jay-Z "American Gangster" CD down as his phone rang again for the fifth time in a row.

"Damn the hoes is ready today, huh?" Whip said, never taking his eyes off the rocks on the chopping block.

"Naw blood, this that bitch ass nigga, Gooney. This nigga think he Frank Lucas or some muthafucking body. We should be the ones running this bitch. This nigga don't even know how to go to war. I told the nigga I'ma stay on point, and he was acting all goofy in front of his dude. His man was on point, though."

Fella dumped another load of product into a pamper.

"This gone be the batch of all batches too, nigga. All we got to do is find out who he cop from, and it's good," Fella said, drying his hands.

Malikie nodded his head as his cell phone went off again.

"Shhhhh," he said, holding up his hand to silence the room.

"Let me see what this nigga wants. I swear he worse than a bitch."

Everyone laughed as Malikie flipped his Metro open.

"What's good, cuz?"

"Why you ain't been answering the phone, nigga? You know y'all are already late." Gooney screamed.

Malikie rolled his eyes as he held one of the packages Carlos was bagging up in his hand.

"I know, big homie, but we almost done, now. We just got two more zips to go."

"Well, hurry up. I just left the block, and Toot say they need more product. You niggas is holding up my money."

Malikie looked at the phone as Gooney continued to rant.

"Big homie, you breaking up. You know how these metros be. I'll hit you in a minute."

Malikie hung up the phone before Gooney could say another word.

"See what I'm saying? This nigga is on some other shit. My niggas, as soon as I find out where this fool cop from, I'ma hurry up and get this clown out the way. You niggas with me when it goes down? Y'all already know how I operate. I don't eat unless my dogs do."

"You know I'm with it," Whip said, as everyone else agreed. Beth came to the doorway and stood with her eyes on the product. Malikie smiled, running his tongue over the gold and diamonds covering his teeth.

"Oh yeah, she on like shit. Was it good, Auntie?"

Beth nodded her head as she scratched her afro.

"Goddamn nephew, you need to let me get a few more of them. That was the best batch y'all done made in a minute. Can I please have some more?"

Malikie laughed as Fella held his arms over his head.

"I'm the champ, nigga! It ain't a muthafucka in the whole Bay that got a whip game like me. Please believe it!" he said, shaking his dreadlocks.

Malikie relaxed and leaned back with his hands behind his head as he thought about taking over the whole operation while everyone laughed and continued their conversation. Turning his head watching Beth eyeball the goods, a surge of power ran through his veins as he handed Beth five more rocks.

"Smoke it up now, Auntie. In a minute there won't be any left."

"Italy, where the hell are my keys? I gotta get out of here.

This cat is expecting me in 20 minutes."

Donovan tossed everything visible around, looking for his car keys.

Italy came downstairs in a silk nightgown with her hair lying smooth and flat across her shoulders. Her nipples stood like small soldiers, poking out of the silk. With everything in place, Italy expected her plan to tame Donavan to work.

"Baby, I have them right here."

Donovan turned around and looked her up and down.

"What are you doing? I just finished fucking you an hour ago. I gotta go now."

Italy threw the keys across the room.

"I want you to make love to me. I want you to feel the passion and warmth of my body. I want you to caress me and let me know you love me. I want you to treat me right. I want you to stay home with me tonight."

Italy placed Donovan's hand on her breast and hers in his crotch.

"I want to talk to you. I want you to listen. After I'm done, you can do what you want, but I have things I need to say. If you love me like you say you do, you'd stop everything and just listen."

Italy was trying hard to be a good woman to Donovan but her childish ways were beginning to wear on him.

Donovan rolled his eyes and pushed her away.

"I gotta go get this money right now. I'll be back in two hours. We can talk then. Cook something and we'll do the whole love thing. Shit, that Chanel stuff you wear ain't cheap."

Italy put her hands on her hips.

"Donovan, I don't care about this shit. Will you stop thinking the world revolves around you for one fucking minute and realize you have a girl at home who needs you?"

Donovan grabbed his keys off the floor as Italy stood directly behind him. Donovan turned around and pushed her in the face.

"Do what I told you, and I'll be back in a minute!"

Italy caught herself from falling. Donovan slammed the door and got into his car. Italy ran behind him and threw a bottle of orange juice at the back of his window as he began to drive off. Donovan hit the brakes and put the car in reverse. Italy matched his icy mug as she stood with her hands on her hips.

"Bitch, you better check yourself. Get the fuck back in the house before I get out of this car and put you back in there. You know you don't want that."

Italy felt the tears begin to burn down her face.

Donovan put the Mustang in drive and screeched out of the complex.

Italy sat down on the curb, holding her face in her palms as the cold of the morning slid down her spine, causing her to tense up. Beth suddenly crossed her mind. She ran inside, poured a glass of Moet, and dialed the number. The glass trembled in her hand as she waited for Beth to pick up.

"Hello," Beth said laughing.

"Momma, how are you doing?"

"Italy? I was wondering when your ass would call. Where are you?"

"I'm at home, if that's what you want to call it. I was thinking about you. How is everything?"

"Everything is the same. I'm just over here cooking. Bobby is over here."

"That's good. Momma, if I wanted to come home, do you think it would be cool?"

A long silence stretched between them as Beth ran the thought of having her daughter back home through her head.

"I don't know, Italy. You don't want to listen to nobody, and I'm enjoying my space. Plus, Bobby doesn't want you here and he pays the bills, so no. It wouldn't be cool."

Italy let the phone drop from her ear as she slammed it down on the base and began crying.

Savoring the taste of the champagne, Italy swallowed slowly before rage engulfed her and she threw the glass at the wall. Both she and the glass shattered as she slumped against the counter.

"Why the fuck is this happening to me?" she screamed to the silent room.

Wiping her eyes, Italy dug through her CD case until she found her Isley Brothers CD. "You Deserve Better," came smooth over the speakers as Italy gathered herself and rolled a joint. Quickly, she cleaned the glass up, and poured another as she lit the joint and sat on the leather couch, letting the music massage her soul and take her to another place. Italy wrapped her arms around herself and rocked back and forth, while drifting off on different memories.

Kamal, popped up and lingered for a second, but was quickly dismissed with the thought of their last conversation. She put the song on repeat and stared at the wall. Jason suddenly popped into her head as she realized she hadn't picked up the book he had given her, but instead tried to manipulate Donovan's mind. Italy took two more pulls from the joint and downed the glass of champagne.

First, she picked up the phone and called Tanya. Italy pulled out her Coach bag and retrieved the book after Tanya wasn't home. Turning the CD player off, she desperately tried to clear her mind. *Read this with a clear head,* she kept repeating to herself. Italy closed her eyes and let all the things she'd been thinking about flow from her body as she opened the book and started chapter one.

Italy lost track of time and hadn't moved. She realized hours had passed, when Donovan walked in. She jumped when the door slammed and broke her concentration, as Donovan walked past her upstairs. She cut her eyes at him as he walked by, without saying a word. A faint smell of perfume not her own, lingered in his wake.

Italy gritted her teeth and flung open the book as the

shower started upstairs.

Donovan came back down stairs after he showered.

"What's up baby?" he said, slapping her feet.

Italy pulled her knees into her chest.

"Donovan, please don't touch me. What do you want? I'm trying to get into this book."

Donovan blew out a long, hard breath.

"Whatever, nigga! What did you cook? I'm hungry as hell."

Italy remained silent.

Donovan tapped her on her legs.

"Did you hear me? Go on with all that silent, quiet shit, Italy. I had to handle some business, okay? So check that snotty ass attitude at the door."

"Donovan, I didn't cook anything. I know you didn't expect me to, with you pushing me in my face and all. Why don't you go have that bitch you were just fucking cook for you? I'm sure she's better since you keep spending all your time with her, *or them*, or whatever."

Donovan stood frowning at her as she didn't look up from her book. Italy stopped reading and focused her eyes on one word, waiting for his reaction. Donovan let an evil smile creep across his face. He snatched the book out of Italy's hand and read the cover.

"The *Art of War*? Who you trying to go to war with? Yo' stupid ass trying to learn something, huh?"

Italy sat with her arms now wrapped around her knees. Donovan threw the book down.

"Get your ass up and cook something. Don't forget who's taking care of you and who's paying these bills. You ain't got no place questioning me about shit. So get up and cook some food. I'm not going to tell you again."

Italy began rocking and humming to herself, making Donovan even more frustrated when she didn't move. He leaned forward and slapped her viciously across the face. Italy fell back across the couch as Donovan proceeded to smack her repeatedly. Italy screamed and tried fighting back, but his weight and power on top of her was just too much. Struggling only made him hit harder. Italy stopped fighting and suddenly lay motionless. She couldn't feel the smacks anymore and could no longer hear Donovan's grunts as he swung with all his might.

Donovan stood back, pulled her by the ankles off the couch, and kicked her repeatedly. Italy never responded, causing Donovan to stop. He stood over her, feeling winded as he fought for words to say.

"Bitch, don't you ever bite the hand that feeds you. When I tell you to do something, you get your ass up and do it. Now get up and cook something. Don't make me tell you again, either."

Italy lay on the floor, not wanting to fight anymore.

"Okay baby," she whispered.

Donovan sat down and turned the television on as he emptied a baggie of coke onto the glass coffee table.

Italy picked herself up and staggered to the kitchen. She pulled a pot from under the sink and ran hot water into it.

"Is spaghetti fine, Donovan?"

"Hell yeah, put a lot of meat in it," he said, turning the channel to BET.

Italy wiped a tear from her face as she turned on the fire to the stove. Playa Circle's "Duffle Bag Boy" video came on as Italy broke up the spaghetti noodles. She glanced at the TV, secretly wishing she was one of the video girls. The thought of being free and enjoying herself made her realize more than ever that she didn't deserve this. Love seemed a long, hard walk home, in the middle of an Arizona summer.

Italy put a pound of ground beef into a pan of onions and bell peppers. As she seasoned and stirred the meat, she suddenly wished she was on her period, so she could mix the blood in with his portion. The thought made her smile.

Donovan was immersed in snorting as much coke as he

could when the phone suddenly rang.

Donovan pushed her back into the kitchen when she attempted to run to the cordless phone. Donovan jumped faster as he wiped the dust from his nose.

"Cook the damn food, I got it."

Italy turned around and balled her fists as Donovan spit into the receiver. "Who is this?" she heard him scream. The cocaine was obviously beginning to take effect.

"What do you want?"

Italy knew it was Tanya returning her call.

Donovan pinched his nose as he held the phone to his ear.

"Naw, she'll call you back. She's cooking. Don't call, she'll call you."

Donovan hung up and grabbed a bottle of juice out of the refrigerator. "Tell your friend not to call over here anymore. You call her. Really, I don't want you hanging with her. She's a hoe, for real. I don't like her at all. Stay away from her."

Italy slammed the spoon down on the counter.

"Damn it, Donovan! You can't control my friends. You can't stop Tanya from calling me. That's my sister. You know what-"

"I know what?" Donovan cut in. "Bitch, I'm tired of arguing with you. You can leave anytime you want. There's another bitch that'll replace you right now." Donovan turned the TV off. "I ain't hungry no more. Do what you want, Italy. I'm gone. I got some shit to do. If you gone when I get back, peace. But you and I both know your ass will be right here. What you gone do, run back to yo' dope fiend ass momma?"

Donovan grabbed his keys and coat before slapping Italy on the butt and kissing her neck.

Italy turned the food off and sat on the couch, while Donovan laughed at her as he walked out the door. Pulling at her hair and rubbing her shaking hands over a tear stained face, Italy quickly got up and changed her clothes. Italy's body shook out of control as she put on a waist length leather coat and Nike Air Jordans over Miss Sixty jeans. A Nike hat pulled down low over her eyes hid the fear and desperation scribbled across her face as she called Tanya.

"TeeTee, I need you to come and get me. I'll be waiting outside. You don't even need to call, just come and get me please. If you can't, call me back"

Italy hung up the phone and grabbed her keys and stash of weed. Without any thought, she went into the closet and lifted up Donovan's floorboard. She took out $700.00, screaming on the inside, but still leery of taking anything.

Chapter 16

Italy left the house, hoping Tanya was on her way as she walked to the corner liquor store.

"Gimme two packs of Black & Milds and a bottle of Hennessey, please," she said standing at the counter, hiding her face from the clerk.

"Italy, what's up girl?" The store owner, Juice, asked. "You look like you're going through it. Is everything all right?"

Italy exhaled, shaking her head.

"Not really, Juice."

Juice sat his big, black, sweaty frame in a chair too small for his 300lb. body, as he ran a damp rag over his fat face. His dark skin shined bright from the sweat as he wiped again, taking breaths between every word.

"You know you're too fine and sweet to be stressing. Holla if you want to. I'm all ears."

Italy grabbed her bag, staring with a look of disgust for a second.

"Naw, Juice, I'm cool. You run your mouth too much. I don't need the whole city knowing my business."

Juice let out a low grunt and giggle. His whole body shook when he did.

"Shit, I don't be telling anybody anything. You better send that to someone else. I make sure you bitches ain't playing my niggas, coming in here with different cats. You cool. I ain't got nothing to say."

Italy threw up her hand as she walked out.

"Maybe if yo' niggas acted right, there would be no problems. You heard the song, 'Treat 'Em Right, Nigga'."

Juice laughed harder as Italy let the doors swing shut.

She rolled her eyes and felt more enraged.

"All these nigga's ain't shit," she said to herself as she pulled her hat down lower and waited for Tanya to pull up.

As the sun went down, Italy's mind drifted past everything she was seeing. She imagined herself alone on a beach, feet buried in the sand, as the waves ran over her, under the hot fire of the sun. The man of her dreams ran up behind her and scooped her into his arms as she stared in a trance at the sidewalk.

Tanya's horn blaring brought her back to reality.

"Girl, get your high ass in the car. You sitting out here stuck and shit." Tanya yelled out her window, laughing.

The sight of Tanya made Italy warm on the inside.

"What's up, girl?" Italy said, getting into the car.

"Damn, what you got, Henney and blunts? What the fuck the nigga do this time? He was rude than a muthafucka on the phone"

Italy sank into her seat.

"Tanya, girl, I'm so sick of this. The fool put his hands on me again. I wanted to just chill with him and he flipped. I gotta get out of there."

Tanya stopped at a red light.

"Italy, what's keeping you there? Bounce. Fuck these insecure ass niggas, wanting women to be their mommas. It's way too much to life, to even limit yourself to that."

"I know, TeeTee, but what am I going to do? Live in a shelter? Never that! I thought of something, though. I want to know if you'll be down with me."

"What you got in mind? You know I got your back through anything."

Italy smiled and gave her some dap.

"Okay, peep this. You already know what Donovan does, but you don't know how much money he has stacked. TeeTee, it's at least 80 thousand. He has that, and some dope in a floorboard in the house. I was thinking we could get that and shake the spot. Me and you. Fuck these niggas. All they do is lie, cheat, and treat us like shit. Fuck it, why can't we do it back? Especially a nigga wide open as Donovan.

"This fool got sprung on the pussy and put me up in a spot with all that doe. The way he treated me when I gave his ass a chance and my time-I got to get him. I ain't even fucked nobody else since I been with him. I'll be damned if I go out like that. Today, I felt like the weakest chick on the planet. After he whupped me, I did exactly what he told me to do. It's like I was hypnotized and only what he said mattered. I would've dropped to my knees if he told me to. That's how out of it I was. When he left, I snapped back and looked at myself in the mirror. I don't even want to think about it. All I want to do is think about the money we can get, and getting away. So are you with me?"

"Hell yeah! My momma and daddy have been tripping lately, anyway. I wish I knew something about dope, so we can get that too. Just completely strip his ass. Fuck it, we gone take that too. I know who to ask about it."

"Who? We don't really know anybody."

"Shelia. She'll know. We gotta go get some weed from her anyway, so we can ask her how much the shit goes for."

"I don't even know how much it is. I think I heard him say a kick stand or some shit."

"A kick? Girl, that's a kilo! I learned that from E-40's CD. I always hear rap niggas talking about kicks, so I guess they cost hella money. Let's do it. We can go get the shit now."

"Naw, we going to do it tomorrow night. I'm going to act like everything is cool, and fuck the shit out of him. I'm a suck the water out of his dick. Whenever I put it on him like that, he passes out hard. An earthquake won't wake him up. I'm a bag all the money up while you come get me. Be outside at like 11. It'll be even better if he doesn't come home. Where do you want to go?"

"I don't know. How about down south or something. I know it has to be somewhere popping. If he ain't home when I drop you off, put all your clothes in my car tonight, all right?"

"Hell yeah. Hey, why don't you call one of your dudes and tell them to bring a cute friend. I want some dick tonight. I'm horny just thinking about this."

"I know this cat that's perfect. He and his boy got big ass dicks."

"How do you know what his boy is working with?"

Tanya licked her lips and smiled.

"I'm strong enough to handle two. Sometimes one ain't enough," she said, and they both broke into laughter.

Chapter 17

Gooney lit a blunt as the sweat of passion and hot sex dripped from his chin. The wall heater in the Econo Lodge suite burned on high, causing the sex to be even more intense

Karin lay next to him, stroking his thigh, loving the smooth texture of Gooney's skin, and the calm demeanor he presented during their interactions. It had been three weeks since they met again at Uncle Roy's, a local bar and pool hall that Gooney frequented every weekend to sharpen his pool game. Upon first word, Karin felt herself hypnotized by the confidence and security exploding from his swagger. Gooney was a gentle talker with the women, and listened to their every word, luring them in to do whatever he wanted, leaving him to be one of the most sought after hustlers in the city.

Karin shivered as Gooney ran his fingertips over her back

"What are you thinking about?" he asked, inhaling the purple weed smoke.

Karin was silent as she thought about the blissful feeling she was experiencing now, compared to the scared for her life, firecracker temper Donovan had. But still, Donovan was the man she loved and would do anything for, so the feeling was temporary, and purely lustful.

Gooney blew a mouthful of smoke to the ceiling as Karin held his dick in her hand.

"I'm thinking about how the hell you do what you do with

this thing. I can't believe I let you stick this in my ass."

Gooney laughed as Karin's gentle strokes caused him to harden again. Gooney took her hand and put it on his chest, trying to resist the urge to fuck her again.

"You don't like that?" Karin said, sitting up on the bed.

Gooney blew another ring of smoke as he passed her the blunt.

"Naw, it ain't that, baby. A nigga is just tired, that's all. All that ass you got will drain a nigga for days. I still got money to get, love."

"Hmmm," Karin said, cutting her eyes at him as Gooney put his hands behind his head.

"That's what I'm trying to do my damn self. I just got another job as a correctional officer. I have to go to the academy in two weeks. I'ma be ballin' on you niggas in a minute. Fresh Benz and everything."

Gooney laughed as sparks went off in his head. He loved what he was hearing, and wanted to use the situation to his advantage.

"Is that right? I'm feeling that! I'm digging what I been seeing out of you as of late. You ain't the same from when we used to get down. You getting ya' grown woman on, and that's the business. So you want to retire from that?"

"I think so. Shit, they say the job is way easy. All I gotta do is tell the niggas to go to they cell."

"You don't worry about seeing the niggas you used to fuck with in the game?"

"Hell naw! I'm out getting money and they stuck. So I couldn't give a fuck less."

Gooney took a sip of water from a bottle of Aquafina sitting on the nightstand as he fumbled over the thought of using Karin for another part of business, since profits in prison were four times better than anything on the streets. The shake from a bag of weed was worth the price of a real bag, alone.

Karin smoked the blunt down to the roach as she tossed around her next move. Knowing Donovan wanted to know who his partner was, Karin decided to pillow talk.

"So how are you doing in the game, baby? I see you stepped it up and copped that 745 sitting out there."

Gooney rubbed his chest with pride.

"Oh, the game is good. You know I'm running shit? I got that nigga Donovan out the way, so me and my team eating like crazy. You know how I do it, baby," he said, pushing to make himself bigger.

Karin leaned across his chest as Gooney slapped her on the butt and watched the jiggle.

"Damn, I love this shit here though, girl," he said, slapping it again.

Karin giggled.

"You know this is all yours. You doing yo' thang and I'm about to be doing mine, so I don't need anyone else. Plus you dick a bitch down right."

"That's what I'm trying to hear. You know we can get this money and stunt on niggas real tough. All you gotta do is stay down."

"I'm with it baby, just say the word. Will it be me and you?"

"No doubt! I don't have no partners any more. I run this shit now, and niggas have to answer to me. All you gotta do is listen to what I tell you. Ain't no partnership sweetie, just do what the fuck I tell you, cause I ain't gone tell you nothing wrong. Everything I tell you to do is gonna be for the best. You dig?"

"I feel it, Goon, but you have to listen to me on some things too. You know we women have that intuition. You say you run it now? You had a partner at first?"

Gooney laid his head deep into the pillow as he thought about Jason and the extremes he went to, to go against his best friend for power.

"Yeah," he said solemnly.

"Me and my nigga, Jason, started this shit together. He got out of it though. Said he didn't want it anymore. He was the brains and the nigga with the connection. I met the connect a couple times before he wanted out. Jay is a cautious nigga like that. He don't trust anybody. But that is the past, and this is now. The now is, we get money. My desert eagle is the only muthafucking thing I trust, so don't even think about crossing me."

Karin smiled devilishly as Gooney gave up the information she wanted to hear. She bypassed the threat just made, figuring any man that'll give up info the way he did, is a man asking to get hit. Now the only thing she juggled in her head was if Jason had anything to do with Donovan losing his turf.

Chapter 18

Jason sat at his kitchen table oiling his .55 Caliber Desert Eagle. A cigarette burned in the ashtray as Miles Davis' "Bitches Brew" played in the CD player. Sheila had left early that morning to pick up Fina and run other errands. After he put the gun back together, a skill learned on the internet, he loaded it, and put it back in its case.

Jason's body suddenly turned hot. The recent stresses seemed to weigh him down, and nightmares occurred almost every night, reaching a point where sleep was rare. Most nights were spent tossing and turning, watching Sheila sleep. Never wanting to bother her with it, for it seemed she was sleeping peacefully, for both of them.

Sweat began to trickle down from Jason's forehead, as he rushed to the bathroom and tossed cold water on his face.

"What the hell is going on with me?" he said to himself.

Jason continued splashing the water on his face as he heard a knock at the door. Slowly, he grabbed a towel and stutter stepped to the door. With no shirt and a pair of Sean John shorts hanging past his Sean John underwear, Jason stood to the side and peeped out of a crack in the blinds. Two females stood at the door looking out at the parking lot.

"Who the hell is this?" he wondered.

Slowly opening the door, Jason stood wiping the remainder of the water from his face.

"Can I help you?" he said to the thick brown-skinned girl, watching the other one, as he felt his face become stone.

"When are you going to stop following me?" Jason said to Italy before Tanya could answer.

Italy formed a diamond cutting smile on her face.

Tanya looked at the two of them confused.

"You two have been seeing each other? Italy you ain't told me? Oh you know we gotta talk later."

Jason switched his eyes back to Tanya who was now looking him up and down.

"What do y'all want?"

"Damn," Tanya said. "How're you doing? I'm fine, and you?"

Jason wiped a trickle of sweat from his face.

"I don't have time for this right now. Sheila isn't here. Call her later on."

Italy shook her head.

"You haven't started on that attitude yet, huh? Jason, we just wanted to get some more weed and ask her about something."

"How much weed do y'all need?" Jason asked, frustrated.

"Can we get two ounces please?" Tanya asked, sucking her teeth.

Jason looked her up and down.

"You might want to calm your nerves, sis. You came to my door needing something. Now, which do you want? Purple or green?"

"Purple!" they both said in unison.

"Give me $300.00, and that's love too."

Italy dug in her purse for the money.

Jason put his hand on her arm.

"Hold on! I don't do business like that. How do you two even know where I live?"

Italy and Tanya followed him into the apartment. Their jaws dropped when they entered the cleanliness and beauty of the condo. The whole living room was white and spotless. A flat screen TV hung from the wall with a huge sound system below it. The leather love seat and couch had three white leather pillows across them and the recliner looked as if it hadn't been sat in.

"Sit down at the kitchen table," Jason said. "And don't touch anything!" he screamed as he vanished into the bedroom, leaving them speechless.

"Damn they're doing it big, huh?" Tanya said. "They got real class. Look at all this stuff. They're in stupid love. Look at that picture."

Italy turned to look at the huge pencil drawn picture of Jason and Sheila, suddenly leaving her feeling envious of Sheila and wanting Jason more.

"Jason got body too, huh?" Tanya whispered. "Why you ain't tell me you been seeing him?"

"I haven't. We just always seem to bump into each other ever since that night he gave me a ride home."

Tanya sucked her teeth.

"I don't like his attitude, though. He acts like everything is a problem, and it ain't even cute."

"It has to be for a reason. I can't see anybody just being an ass. He has a soft spot, though. Life is cold ain't it? Maybe that attitude keeps the bullshit away."

"Damn Italy, you feeling that nigga, huh? You sittting here taking up for him. Why don't you ask him about that kick? He is a D-Boy."

Jason walked back into the room with a Ziploc bag of weed.

"What did you need to ask Sheila? I'll find out anyway, so shoot."

Italy handed him the money and put the weed in her purse.

"How much money can we get for a kick?" Tanya asked.

Jason looked at them with a surprised expression.

"Cat got your tongue? You are always straight to the point, so don't act shocked," Italy said.

Jason bit his bottom lip as he stared at her.

Italy's face became somber.

"$16,000.00." Jason said, voice and eyes steady.

Tanya waved her hand between them.

"Hello!" Tanya said. "Do you want to buy one?"

Jason cut his eyes at her.

"No, I don't sell drugs."

Tanya laughed out loud.

"Jason, I'm not the police, nigga. It's just that we're about to come into one, and I don't know how to get rid of it."

"Well, I don't need it. What do y'all have going on?" asked Jason.

Italy pursed her lips. "Do you know a dude named Donovan?"

Jason raised his eyebrows.

"Stupid ass Donovan from Tyrell Ave? Drives a black Mustang?"

"Yeah, that's him. Why do you call him stupid?" Italy asked.

"He's a silly dude. He is in it for the hype, and not the money. That isn't hustling. You hustle to live, pay bills and be comfortable. Investments and opportunities. Not to buy out the bar at a club and act silly as hell, drawing attention to yourself. So yeah, he's silly in my eyes."

"That's her boyfriend," Tanya said, smiling.

Jason shook his head and smiled.

"So that's who's been stressing you out? Now I understand. Do you two have someone set up to buy it?"

"No, not yet. Do you know anyone who might want it?"

Jason looked into Italy.

"Are you sure you want to get into this? I don't think this is your cup of tea. You can't have any weaknesses, grinding."

Tanya rolled her eyes.

"Jay, we'll be all right. Just hook us up with someone to sell it to."

Jason threw his hands up.

"I'll tell you what. Call Sheila when you get the thing, and I want 25% for hooking it all up"

"How much is that?" Tanya asked disturbed.

"Damn sweetie, what did you go to school for? Nothing is free, so don't act surprised. 25% of 16,000 is 4,000. If you get it, we'll sell it for 13,500. So that'll be 3,375 for my cut. So you two do what you do and get back at me. Watch yourself, because taking a nigga like Donovan's money is like taking his livelihood. Be smart and get out of town as soon as you do it."

"Jason, do you want to be a part of it?" Italy whispered.

Tanya looked at her with surprise. She couldn't believe Italy had just invited Jason to be a part of their business.

"No, we don't need his help," Tanya barked. "We can handle this shit ourselves."

Jason smirked.

"Baby girl, I'm not trying to be a part of that, anyway. I'm paid. Your little chicken head attitude and sudden burst of courage will get the two of you killed. This is not Thelma and Louise. What kind of guns do you have?"

Italy looked up at him with a wrinkled face. "Guns? We don't have any and we don't need any."

"Okay, if you get caught, what are you going to do? Cry your way out of it? Try to suck his dick real quick? Please! Donovan isn't that stupid. He'll put a bullet in the both of you. So you better rethink this."

Italy became outraged.

"There's nothing to rethink Jason. You don't know the things that nigga does to me." Italy thought about it. "No, fuck him! Can you hook us up with some heat?"

Jason rubbed his hand over his chin.

"I'll tell you what. I want no parts of it, but I know someone who will be down for it. You will have to cash him out more than 25% because I know you are leaving out one thing."

"What's that?" Tanya said, upset.

"The money! If a nigga has kicks lying around, he has money also. You guys are amateurs, trying to play in the pros. How much money is it?"

"Close to 100,000." Italy said quickly.

Tanya slapped her on the arm.

Jason's eyes widened.

"Oh yes, my boy will be down with that. When are you trying to do this?"

Tanya exhaled loudly.

"In two days. We were going to do it tonight, but we don't want to hold onto that dope."

"Okay, close to $100,000.00, huh? Give my boy $30,000.00 and he'll make sure nothing bad happens to you. Y'all won't have to mess up your pretty little manicures trying to shoot a gun you don't know how to use. Call me tomorrow night. I'll have already talked to my boy, and we'll take it from there."

"Okay," Italy said, standing up.

Jason walked them to the door. Tanya walked out first as Jason grabbed Italy's arm. He stared at her before leaning in close and whispering to her. "I'm going to help you with this, but this ain't you. I can see past the front. Take that money and get into something legit. You are not stupid. Have you been reading that book I gave you?"

Italy nodded her head and whispered, "Yes."

"Be smart girl, this ain't you." Jason stepped back and looked deeply into her eyes.

Italy's knees became weak.

"Thank you Jason," she whispered, barely audible. "I'll call you in the morning." Italy said as she leaned in and tried to kiss his cheek.

Jason put his hand up and blocked it.

"Don't try that again. A simple hand shake will do."

Italy felt embarrassed and quickly stood back.

"We'll talk in the morning," Jason said, backing into the door and shutting it.

Italy looked at the door for a moment before easing down the stairs.

Chapter 19

Later that night, Jason blew smoke from his Newport into the ceiling as he sat low in a 1972 cutlass in front of the strip club, Centerfolds, in San Francisco. He pulled his black 49ers hat down low over his eyes as Savion laid back in his seat, slowly blowing smoke from his nostrils. His black hooded sweatshirt fitted baggy over his large frame. The Jacka "Have you eva" played low over the speakers, spilling out the feelings of every young Bay area hustler.

Savion kept his eyes on the door of the club.

"Jay, do you want to know one thing that I thought about daily while I was in the pen?"

Jason glanced over at him.

"What's that?"

"Why is it that we keep more faith in our guns than in God? I didn't tell you this, but I actually tried to get into God. I went to church a few times, but I didn't feel comfortable. I guess my demons were getting to me, or something. I don't know, but I tried. The more right I tried to live, the more wrong I felt. I just decided that when God is ready for me, he'll call. Maybe Momma will whisper in his ear to touch me. Jay, why don't you ever talk about Momma? You were there with her and there are things I don't know that I want to know."

Jason inhaled the cigarette.

"I don't like to think about it. I try to push her dying out of my head. You don't want to know how it was, Sav. Watching someone die from AIDS is not pretty. She looked so bad. Sheila had to force me into the hospital at times. Momma weighed like 100 pounds when she died, if that, really! Sav, all she talked about was you. How we need to stay tight and you need to get your shit together. I promised her I'd look out for you, but you are making that hard as hell."

"Jay, you're right but it's like evil lives in me. It's so hard to shake this shit, man." Wiping his bro, he turned his back to Jason.

"Sav, look at me, you have got to start thinking before you do shit. Maybe you should've kept going to church, but I understand. There isn't any sense in fronting. The fact that you went, means God is trying to reach you. Your anger is preventing it, though. I think it's time to get over our childhood and your pops. Fuck him! You're not gaining anything off it by constantly tripping. I don't even talk about mine. I'm just thankful for everything I have. That's why I'm done selling coke."

"Yeah right, that shit pulls you in just like it does me. How can you live this lifestyle behind? It's all we know."

"Shut up, Sav. This ain't all we know. Momma did a good job showing us there was another way and you know it. Everything comes to an end one day, so I want to try and live as correct as possible until that day comes. If niggaz kept faith in God, I mean true faith, there wouldn't be any need for a gun. I try to keep true faith, but the life that I live calls for a gun. When me and Sheila move out to the valley, I'm not riding around with one. Shit, I'm not even trying to steal cable. I want to be completely clean. All this is a headache, Sav. Look at us; we're waiting to take someone's life. I understand why, but think about what we could be doing if you didn't put yourself in that position in the first place. We could be kicked back drinking something, laughing over a meal. After this, I mean it Sav, I'm done with it."

Savion continued to let the smoke flow.

"Jay, I can't even say I'm done. I'm not good at anything else. This shit here is all I know, and truthfully, I love it. You can do all that square shit because you're into it. Shit, I have to force you to keep that jazz out of the deck. But me, I'm a gangsta. I'ma get it or die trying. I don't know if I'll go tomorrow, but I at least want to go knowing that I tried to get it instead of lying down not doing anything. Momma raised us that way, Jay. She slung pussy just to survive. I'm a product of the same thing. Survival.

"How can I ever feel cool when I hate what's in me? That muthafucka is on a hill chilling with his little white family, while I'm down here going through shit a man shouldn't have to go through. It's cool to fuck a black woman, but when something is conceived from it, it's all of a sudden, 'that baby ain't mine. Let me go back to my perfect life with picket fences and pink kids.' Fuck that! I'll never get over that shit. Especially with what just happened to me. If I ever see him, Jay, I swear I'm going to unload every bullet in my gun into his pale ass. That's my word!"

Jason stared at Savion as the neon lights illuminated his scarred face and highlighted his anger.

"I gotta survive, Jay," he said, swinging his head around to meet Jason's eyes.

"You did your thing, and luckily never got busted for it. It's my turn, Jay. I deserve my damn turn! Maybe that cold muthafucka up there in the sky will realize that and finally give in, but I deserve my turn."

Savion stopped to inhale his cigarette.

"Now these muthafuckas in here delayed that and violated me in the process. I'll be damned if I tuck my balls between my legs and run. I ain't about to start running from these niggas, man. You did your thing Jay, but don't knock me for how I do mine."

"I'm not knocking you, Sav." Jason said. "I'm saying you

need to clean it up and do it a lot smoother. You've taken all these punches from the game, and don't have a thing to show for it. All I'm saying is, *think*. Think before reacting foolishly. I hope you do have your turn. Maybe all this shit will come to an end when you do. I even set up some shit to help get you there. You'll get 30,000 for it."

Savion's face brightened up.

"What're you talking about? Thirty racks? What do I have to do?"

"Nothing," Jason said flatly.

"All you have to do is ride with these chicks and make sure nothing happens to them. They're robbing this cat for all his money and dope. They're beginners, so I told them you would hold the heat and make sure they make it back to the car and house safely. I have this cat on line for the dope, plus you will get a cut out of that."

Savion smiled ear to ear.

"That's what I'm talking about. When is this going down?"

"It should be in a few days. I'm waiting for her to call me back."

"How much coke is it?"

"They said a kick or two. I don't know. If it is two, I'm going to make them give you one. Plus, I still have that ten for you, so you should be cool."

Savion put up his hand and Jason gripped it tight.

"Good looking out, blood. I'ma flip that real tough. That should put me where I need to be for real."

"I can set you up with some people if you need it, just play it smart and safe."

"I will! If it's pure, I'ma step on it once and break it down in ounces. I heard Reno is cracking real tough right now. I know a cool cat out there that'll help me get it off. I hope the chick calls you soon. I know these muthafuckas here have something too. You didn't register this car did you?"

Jason looked at him with a stupid expression.

"Yeah, I told them your name and what time we were doing this shit. Don't ask me any stupid questions like that."

Savion giggled as he darted his eyes towards the door.

"There they go, Jay. Duck down!"

Savion put his arm on the windowsill as Jason sunk lower in his seat. Fina walked in the middle of the two men with her arm around their waists. She cut her eyes in their direction as she laughed along with the men.

Savion let an evil grin creep across his face.

"They didn't even see us, Jay. Start the car!"

Earlier that day, after combing the streets of San Francisco all day, Savion finally caught up with the right person to point him in the direction to find the guys who violated him. After realizing he was in prison with one of them, it wasn't hard to find him in Fillmore.

After getting the information he needed, Savion followed Bruce, the main bisexual homo-thug, through the streets all day, staying on his every move.

Jason called a meeting at his condo after Savion let him know everything he knew, and organized a plan using Fina as the bait to Bruce and his cronies' bisexual tendencies.

Jason, Savion, and Fina camped out in front of Bruce's apartment in the rough and rugged Page Street projects in the heart of Fillmore until he and his boy, Ike, came out. They followed them through downtown San Francisco until they landed in the city nighttime high life of Broadway, at the strip club. Fina worked her magic, convincing the two to come with her to a hotel for sexual pleasures, something that the two couldn't resist when she flicked her tongue and swayed her phat ass in their faces.

Jason started the car as Fina and the men drove by in a blue Buick. Jason let a few cars pass him by, before pulling into traffic.

"Jay, don't lose them," Savion said, excited.

"Be cool. I got it," Jason said.

"Fina is not going to let them get too far." Savion stretched his neck to make sure he could see them.

Staying two cars back, as they pulled in front of a motel on Turk street, Jason slowed down and watched Fina walk into the motel with the two men. Savion pulled out his .357 Magnum and flipped it open to make sure all the bullets were loaded.

"Wait right here and open the trunk. Fina has her heat on her, right?"

Jason put the car in park in front of the motel.

"Yeah, now hurry up. This spot is not cool."

Savion pulled his hood over his head and tied the strings.

"First room on the second floor, right?"

Jason nodded his head. Savion slammed the door and tucked the gun in his waistband. Jason watched him run in the building and quickly climb the stairs as he got out of the car and opened the trunk. He stood next to the car and watched the prostitutes walk up and down Turk street, stopping at cars. The traffic was thick on the Friday night, as tricks needing pleasures their wives wouldn't provide drove by, consumed by lust.

Turk street, deep in the heart of the dangerous and world-renowned Tenderloin Section of San Francisco, was just like any other bottomless pit of despair in any city in the country. Littered with liquor stores on every corner, mixed with sex shops and hole in the wall strip clubs, the tone was set for the deadly ingredients of sex, drugs, and murder.

A cop car cruised by slowly, meeting eyes with Jason, causing him to tense up, but remain calm. He exhaled and flicked his cigarette away when he saw their lights disappear. He quickly turned around when he heard heels clicking loudly behind him.

Fina came out of the motel, moving fast, holding her gun to her side under her coat.

"Jay, get in the car, baby. Savion has it all covered."

Jason climbed in as Fina got into the backseat.

"Pull out quick too, Jay. This shit is about to look real funny."

Jason put the car in drive with his foot on the brake. As he looked up the street, he saw Savion rushing the two men out of the building naked. He held his gun to Bruce's head and pushed Ike out in front of him. Jason nervously looked around for police. Savion ushered the two men to the trunk and made them get in, slapping Bruce with the butt of the gun before slamming the trunk.

Quickly, he got into the car.

"Drive down to Page Street. This nigga has the loot in the house."

Jason pulled into traffic and quickly got out of everyone's eyesight, riding in silence until they reached Page.

"Okay, the house is two blocks from here. Pull in the front, while I drag this nigga in the house to get the money."

Jason continued driving until he reached the corner. He and Savion got out and opened the trunk, leaving Jason to see the fear on Bruce and Ike's faces as they lay naked next to each other.

The scene disturbed him, but made him laugh at the same time. Savion pulled out his gun and grabbed Bruce, the smaller of the two, out of the trunk. Sweat trickled down his dark face as his eyes bulged out.

"Man, I'll give you all the money I have, just let me get a pass."

Savion slapped him with the gun again.

"Shut the fuck up! Is anyone in the house?"

"Yeah, my girl. Let me go in and get it for you, man."

Savion slapped him again.

"Jay, tell Fina to get in the driver's seat. Come in with me."

Jason shook his head and cocked back his gun as he leaned in the window and gave her the instructions. Bruce started to pee on himself as Jason shut the trunk. Savion laughed as he pushed him up the stairs to the apartment. Jason looked up and down the street, noticing that no one seemed to pay any attention to them. Savion banged on the door with his fist.

"It's me baby, let me in," Bruce said as Savion held the gun to his head.

Jason stood by the side of the door as it opened. A short caramel skinned girl opened the door. Her smile turned to horror when Jason put the gun in her face.

"Shhhh! I won't hurt you if you don't scream," Jason whispered.

The woman backed into the house as they walked in. Tears formed in her eyes as Jason adjusted the bandana across his face.

"Sit down, and nothing will happen to you."

The woman sat down as Savion pushed Bruce to the back of the house. Jason put the gun in his waistband and stood in front of his woman. Savion began yelling, making Jason nervous that he would shoot him there. Bruce's woman looked at the floor, causing Jason to feel bad for her being caught up in something she had nothing to do with.

Savion pushed Bruce back into the living room, holding a duffle bag. "You didn't tie her up?" he asked.

"No, fuck that shit. Let's bounce!"

"Damn, blood," Savion said, stepping behind the woman and knocking her out with the butt of the gun.

The woman slumped to the side and slid onto the floor as they rushed out of the house and back to the car. Jason opened the trunk as Savion forced Bruce back in.

"Damn man, you got what you wanted, now let me get a pass, please!"

Savion pointed the gun in his face.

"Not here!" Jason yelled. "Not here, that's too much attention. Let's drive to a cut."

Savion pulled the gun back and slammed the trunk.

"Drive out by Candlestick," he said, getting back into the car.

Savion turned the music up as far as it would go to flush out their screams.

"When we get there, don't waste any time talking. Put two in them and get back into the car," Jason said.

"I want to torture these fools, Jay. A bullet is too easy."

"Well, a bullet is gonna have to do. We don't have time for all that. I feel you, but we have to do this and get on. That other shit will get us caught up."

Savion smacked his lips and nodded his head. "Aiight, we'll do it like that. I got at least twenty thousand here. It doesn't make up for it, but fuck it."

Fina leaned over the seat. "Jay, what you gonna do with this car?"

"Dump it! It's too hot. I'm going to burn it in the cut somewhere. I don't trust keeping it, or you keeping it."

Fina exhaled and sat back in the seat.

Jason pulled into the parking lot of Candlestick Point, parked in the shadows, and got out of the car. The night hid them well, as the cold March chill and San Francisco winds blended to make a biting cold. Jason opened the trunk and pulled Ike out, as Savion grabbed Bruce. Both men began screaming and crying.

"Shut the fuck up," Savion said, cocking his gun.

Bruce started bobbing up and down as he hollered, suddenly turning around and trying to run.

Savion took off after him as Jason turned to Ike and stuck his gun under his chin.

"Nigga, don't even think about it." Ike swallowed hard and began shaking.

Savion fired the gun one time, catching Bruce in his back thigh. His face scrubbed into the gravel as Savion caught up with him, breathing hard while trying to get out a few words.

"Can't run from this one, baby. Open your fucking mouth!"

Bruce didn't move as he whimpered, holding his thigh.

Savion put the gun between his lips.

"Nigga, ain't this what ya' faggot ass like? You like to suck on dicks and shit, huh? So this shouldn't be nothing, fuckin' homo!"

Bruce whimpered as Savion tried to put the barrel of the 357 further down his throat.

"Yeah, nigga, cry. Maybe God will give yo' bitch ass a pass, but not me. Imagine you staring into the eyes of the devil, nigga," Savion said, pulling the trigger three times.

Blood splattered upwards into his face as Savion smiled and spit on him once. He wiped the blood from his face as Jason held Ike still. Savion saw his knees knocking together.

"Nigga you wasn't scared when you kicked in my door, was you?"

Ike continued shaking. Jason stepped back as Savion put his gun to the side of Ike's head. He didn't blink as he pulled the trigger once, leaving the gun smoking as Ike fell to the ground and Savion released the rest of the bullets into him.

Jason couldn't blink as Savion stared at him in a trance. Fina watched everything from the back seat in awe of the two.

"Let's go," Jason said, getting into the front seat.

Savion spit again on the dead, stiff body and got into the car.

"Keep your gloves on, and don't touch anything in this car without them. Sav, throw those guns into the water right now."

Savion looked at him, dazed and in another world, before getting out of the car and throwing the guns far out into the shallow tide of the bay waters.

"You alright?" Jason said, as Savion got back into the car.

Savion nodded his head as he lit a cigarette without saying another word.

Chapter 20

"Jay, you look like shit," Bino said as they sat in TGI Friday's in Union City.

"I haven't been sleeping well. Is it that bad?"

Bino nodded as he took a bite of his chicken salad.

"Stress is the number one killer. You know that, right?"

Jason shrugged.

"Why are you stressing anyway? You're not in the game anymore and you and Shelia are about to get married. What's the problem?"

"Savion is home."

Bino stopped chewing as he looked at him with worry.

"Oh! What is he doing now?"

"What isn't he doing? Things are hot right now. This fool has popped three people since he has been home."

"Well, why are you letting it stress you out? If Sav wants to keep living the way he is, then let him. You can't make anyone change. They have to want it for themselves. Obviously, he doesn't want it. Jay, you're like a son to me. I'm not trying to be accepting calls from the pen or putting fresh flowers on your gravesite every month. When you were younger, I could tell you what and what not to do. You're grown now. You're the general, and you must start thinking like one.

"Do you know why the majority of people who do what we do are dead? Because they think and do things off of emotions or pride. Sometimes you have to swallow that and think with logic. Thinking irrationally is what brings the pain. Now people might think you're crazy, soft, or whatever, but that's what separates the leaders from the followers. Leaders sometimes may have to accept humility in order to proceed.

"You have a vision of the way you want to live or where you want to be when you reach my age. You have a soldier and someone who loves and will look up to you in Shelia. You have to keep your emotions in check in order to continue to rise above it all. Discipline! I know the situation with Savion, but you can't continue to save someone who wants to die. Right now, I'm sure he doesn't give a fuck about anyone or anything but himself. If he did, he wouldn't have asked you to do the things he has. Shake the emotion, Jay. It will kill you in the long run."

Jason nodded and let out a well-needed breath of air.

"Shelia has been hella mad, lately. This shit has her upset and on the edge. I had this other thing set up with these two chicks robbing their dude. He's a crazy cat, but he ain't crazier than Sav. I let Sav in on it to put some money in his pocket. I'm cool off it all. They can handle it themselves."

Bino talked with his fork.

"That would be the best. Let him find himself. Hopefully he does, before he gets killed. Jason, you're too smart. I taught you better and you listened with all ears. Feel me on this one. You're getting married next week. Start over from that moment. This shit is all behind you. Who's this dude they are talking about robbing?"

"This cat in Union City, nothing to worry about. Bee, for all the shit you talk, why haven't you quit yet? You have more than enough money and a family. You haven't thought about going to the pen or anything?"

"You know what, Jay? I used to, but not anymore. I move in stealth. Shit, you're one of the best, and I taught you. Don't worry about me, Jay. Money makes the world go round, and I have enough to keep me out of jail. I am not tied to any murders or anything. That's why I am telling you to leave Savion alone. Please take my advice."

Jason looked out the window.

"I understand. Shelia has been saying the same thing. I got it under control, man. I gotta think about the fit I'm wearing for this wedding. What do you think about a Polo cream jean suit?"

Bino shook his head, laughing at the question.

"You and this hip hop shit. Try again, Jay."

Jason smiled as he bit into his chicken sandwich.

"Jay, baby, I'm ready to leave. This past month has been crazy. When we were younger and still struggling to get where we are now, I didn't even care. Now that we are here, I just want to live right and enjoy everything we have worked hard for. Are you listening?"

Jason laid in the bed with his arm around Sheila's shoulders as she listened to the beat of his heart. The rain pounded upon the window like light snares as Jason caressed her shoulder in silence.

"Jay, do you hear me?"

Jesse Powell's "I Only Love You" played softly in the background.

Jason kissed her forehead softly.

"I'm ready, been ready. I can't take too many more punches. Look at me, baby, I have been losing weight like crazy and I look like shit. This whole thing with Savion is killing me, plus, I'm about to finish this nigga, Gooney. The cold part is that if I wanted it all, I could get rid of two birds with one stone in Gooney and Donovan, but Donovan has done nothing to me."

Jason rolled out of bed and rubbed his hands over his

face.

"Do you want to take a ride with me real quick? I have something I want to show you."

Sheila looked at him, questioningly.

"What is it? It's one in the morning." Jason stood in front of her as his naked body glowed from the moonlight.

"This is something important I've been wanting to show you for a long time, but just couldn't. Get dressed."

Sheila stood up and kissed his lips softly while Jason massaged the back of her neck.

"Let's go," he said, slapping her butt.

Chapter 21

Jason pulled his Diamante into the parking lot of Arroyo Park in East Oakland. He turned the car off and sat with the windshield wipers on, staring out into the open darkness.

"Jay, I have been here a million times. What's so special about this place?" Shelia asked.

Jason lit a Newport and blew the smoke out quickly.

"I remember when I was little, real little, my daddy used to bring me up here. We used to watch Hot Lips box here. He would throw these little events and knock cats out in the ring. I had never seen anyone with hands like that. Everyone knew my pops. He was like a star. He used to run with Felix Mitchell when they had their thing going. I remember him showing me off. He even embraced Sav like he was his own."

"Awe baby, you are so much like him. So loving and generous with your time. I wished that I would have been able to meet him." Sheila spoke quietly but loud enough for Jason to hear her sweet words.

"My mom was crazy about him. He used to sport those T1 sweat suits with big ass gold chains and shell toes, just a young factor. I remember Short use to sell his tapes out here. It was crazy. Women wore those Chic jeans and big ass doorknocker earrings, peeling their ear lobes off. Gold was everywhere, in their mouth, on their fingers, neck, and wrists. It seemed like it was all love. I use to run around, bad as hell.

Women with all those crazy hairdos would pick me up and kiss me all over. My momma was a star, 'cause all the broads wanted my pops. He drove a Saab and a Jag, looking just like I do now, except he had a curl."

Sheila laughed and knocked if off quickly, knowing Jason was being serious.

"Anyway, we came out here one night. He had to handle some business and had me and Sav with him. He picked up this chick, she was hella fine. He was doing his thing, but mom's was number one. He had a thing for women. I remember me and Sav running around and wrestling. He and the chick sat on the hood of his car smoking a joint. I will never forget, he had on Sergio Valente jeans and a tee shirt. It was hot outside, and me and Sav were rolling around on the ground when I heard a loud pop. I looked up and saw my daddy falling to the ground. I heard it again and again. The chick started screaming real loud, and a dude turned and popped her too. I just sat there looking at him, while he tucked his gun in his pants and ran off."

Sheila almost spoke, but when her lips parted, Jason shushed her.

"I walked over to where my pops was laying. I remember thinking that he was asleep. I shook him hella times, but he didn't move. Blood was pouring from his head like crazy. I had it all over my hands. Savion stood there in shock. He knew what had happened. He started pulling me away from my pops, but I was struggling and crying, then the police and ambulance came in what seemed like hours. Savion and I sat in the car quietly, while he held me in his arms. All I could do was stare at my pop's body. I remember Mom came, and that she went crazy. I live with that all the time. It happened right here in this spot."

"Jason, I can't even imagine. I will never leave you, never hurt you and never forsake our love." They hugged in a tight embrace.

"After that, things were never right. Momma lost it and just went for what she knew. Savion was never the same, he just grew cold. I think because my dad was the first man to love him and treat him like a son. Something his pops never did and wouldn't do. He started to carry hatred towards everything, even the white side of him." Jason became quiet as he stared out of the window.

"What about you? How did you feel," asked Sheila.

"I got quiet. I would not talk much, did what I was told, and clung to my momma. She laced me on the basics of the game in her spare time. She used to always tell me to read and write down what I was feeling, since I wouldn't talk much. I used to catch a bus out here late at night and whisper a conversation with Pops. It seemed like he heard me because I always seemed to make the right choices afterwards. I remember when I first met Bino. I talked to pops and it was like a green light, and everything has been real cool. Bino is what I think my pops would be like today. I love dude, like he is my pops."

"Jay, why haven't you ever told me about this? We tell each other everything. Why are you telling me now?"

Jason lit another cigarette.

"I don't know. I think this whole thing with Sav has got me tripping. Plus, we are about to get married and I never told you anything about my pops and his death. I think that's why I can't sleep lately."

"You may need to consider seeing a doctor, baby. I think you have insomnia, and plus, you're paranoid."

"I have reason to be. Life expectancy in this game is thin. Sav told me your name was in a lot of people's mouths when he was locked up. I don't know what I would do if anything happened to you."

"I would expect you to keep living, Jay. I know you would respect me in everything you do, just like I'd do if anything happened to you. I would make sure this baby knows who his father was, and is."

Jason looked up through the windshield in shock. Sheila caressed the back of his head. I'm pregnant, Jay. That's why I have been having an attitude lately."

Jason took her hands in his and kissed her palms.

"Does this mean you're happy?" asked Sheila.

Jason kissed them again and then moved to her neck and shoulders.

"Jay, baby, tell me something," she said, holding his face in her hands.

Sheila smoothed Jason's arched eyebrows out and kissed his forehead. The kid within emerged through the frustration and creases of his face.

"You look like you are ten again, in the picture when Rochelle was kissing you. I want our son to be named after you. Lil' Jay is nice."

"Naw," he whispered.

"We have to let him have his own identity. I don't want to overshadow him. We may not even have a boy."

"That might be true, but I feel this baby I am carrying is a boy. I can sense these things. Are you ready to be a daddy, Jay? Do you think you'll love me the same and stay faithful to everything that we have created? I couldn't take that, Jay. I couldn't think straight with you not being here like the way you are now. I promise to be there for your every request and need. I just need you to do the same.

"As we go through this transition, shit is going to get crazy. I have been slowly, but surely, letting go of certain things. I want us to be completely legal. I know we will still smoke weed, but everything else needs to be clean."

Jason just looked at her, feeling weak, as his emotions started to get the best of him. He thought about how his father must have felt when his mother told him that she was pregnant. Thoughts of Savion pulling him away from his dad when he was killed, and his mother silently crying and rocking in her chair while chain smoking, filled his head. The after effect of the situation, and how the so-called friends turned their backs on them, leaving Rochelle to fend for herself the best way she knew how, weighed heavily on him.

"I would never leave you, Sheila. With all the things that I have seen and been through, I couldn't do that. We are going to be all right and make it through whatever. Please don't think any other way. I am here, and will always be here, okay?"

Sheila kissed him softly.

"This blessing we have, has me all emotional. If I just start to cry for no reason, just hold me. Let me get it all out. My mood swings will be crazy."

Jason grinned.

"I can't wait till that ass gets even bigger. Can I suck some milk too? You are going to be getting thicker than before."

"Jay, you hella nasty, you know that you want to do it anyway."

"That might be true."

"I am going to need a lot of foot massages and things. Sex will be a little boring when I start bulging. I know I'm gonna be humongous. We're both big and tall."

"Shit, we will be set for life. NBA or the NFL is a must."

"What happened to the own identity thing?"

"It's still there, but we can't let all that size go to waste."

"Jay, I registered at Chabot. I want to get started on school, now. I am taking the GED test in two days. I've been studying like hell. I have been going to the library, that's what I have been doing with my free time. I haven't been neglecting you, it's just that I am getting a jump start on our future. When the doctor told me that I was pregnant, things just hit me harder. I want a career and I have decided what I want to do."

"Really, what's that?"

"I want to be a medical assistant. They make good money, and it looks like it's interesting. Have you thought about what you want to do?"

"Pornos!"

Sheila pinched his arm.

"Nigga please, that sword down there will only be pleasing me. But for real, Jay, this is important."

Jason ran his hands over his head.

"I was thinking about being a writer. I have always liked it, and I have written enough poetry. But I want to try to write a book, and see where it will take me. What do you think?"

"I think that it would be off the chain. Your poetry is so deep, already. What would you write about?"

"Life, love and war. That's what we go through on a daily basis. Trying to live life in love is a fucking war. But living and loving you is a battle that I will fight to the end."

Jason smoothed his hand over her cheek and slowly dragged his finger to outline her lips. Sheila sucked them into her mouth and slowly caressed them with her tongue. Jason took off his coat and shirt as Sheila watched him get out the car into the pouring rain. Sheila turned the lights on as he stood in front of the car. The rain ran down his bald head and muscled chest and Jason moved his hand, along with the rain, down to his crotch. As he held his dick and waved his finger at her, Sheila got out and walked slowly around to him.

Jason kissed her tenderly, letting his hands maneuver over her body in a steady motion. He kissed every inch of her upper body as she let out soft moans, pulling his head down to her hard, erect nipples. Jason lightly bit both of them and pulled them gently with his teeth. He sucked and kissed the right one, while massaging the other.

"Jay, I need to feel you, daddy," said Sheila, while trembling.

The rain was a gentle cold pleasure over her heated body. Jason gently laid her back on the hood of the car and kissed her deeply while caressing her thighs.

"How do you feel right now?" asked Jason as he looked into her hazy eyes.

"Lucky. I feel like nothing else matters, but this moment. I am so hot and wet right now."

Jason licked his lips and stuck his hand between her thighs, massaging her spot through her silk panties. He felt her wetness and fingered his way to her clitoris and rubbed slowly.

Sheila let out hard moans as Jason kissed her chin and neck.

"Jay, taste me baby. I need you to taste me."

Jason sped up his motions as he knew she was close to climaxing. He sucked her breasts again and listened as her panting quickened. He snaked his tongue down her stomach and grabbed her by the waist. Sheila sat up, grabbed his head in her hands and began to deeply kiss him as he ran his hands and fingertips lightly on her back. He then proceeded to pull her skirt up and slip her panties off.

Sheila lay back down as he kissed around and between her thighs. She tightened her thighs around his head and caressed her breasts as he ran his tongue around the outside of her pussy. Sheila jumped and grinded her body into his face. Jason knew she was ready to explode. He let her wetness moisten his fingers, as he gently pulled her hood back and rubbed her clitoris.

Jason felt it stiffen as he put her clitoris between his lips and slowly sucked. He then stuck two fingers in her, curling and pumping them slowly. The way he took his time with her body drove her crazy.

"I want you to come hard for me, baby. Can you do that?"

"Ye...ye...yes, Jay. Make me come, baby."

Jason spread her hips apart and started to lick and suck away furiously.

Sheila bucked her body with every motion as he rubbed her clitoris fast, sticking one finger in her butt. Sheila screamed as she exploded all over his face, holding his head tightly between her legs. Jason lapped up every bit of her juices as he continued licking.

"Jay, I'm about to come again, keep going baby."

Jason continued his motions as Sheila banged on the hood of the car, wiggling her body into his face faster as she gripped his head harder. Jason pulled back and let his fingers continue.

Sheila threw her legs up and turned so hard, that Jason thought that she would roll off the car. "Oh God, yes, yes, ye...ye...yes, Lord." Jason's fingers were soaked as she came again.

He pulled them out and stuck them in her mouth. Sheila sucked his fingers, tightly, jerking and moaning, low and deep. He pulled his fingers free and began kissing her deeply. Sheila ran her hands all over his head.

"Fuck me Jay, fuck me hard, baby," she said, while biting his bottom lip.

Jason pulled her off the hood and spun her around. He bent her over. The cold water on her heated body made her scent rise into the mist. Jason bit her shoulder and nibbled on her earlobes.

"You smell so good, babe. You are too beautiful to ever deny. I want you more with each day that passes. You are my lover and down ass bitch, who I can always depend on. How much do you want me?" Jason slowly eased himself into her.

Sheila rotated her bottom in circles until he was all the way in.

"Yes baby, yes. I want you more than words can describe. Fuck me, Jay. Give it all to me, baby."

Jason positioned his hands next to hers on the car and slowly moved in and out of her. Sheila held the back of his head as it rested on her shoulder next to her ear. Both of their soft pants filled their ears. Sheila kissed him deeply as Jason moved faster and he swallowed all her passion as he bit her bottom lip. He pulled away and slapped her butt; Sheila pushed back with his rhythm. Jason leaned forward and played with her love button, keeping his motions firm and in sync.

"Oh my God, oh my God, Jay I am comin' hard.

Fu…fu…fuckkkk." Jason pulled her body close and tight to his.

Sheila liked it when he made love to her from behind and made her climax. Sheila's body jerked and jerked as Jason slowed his rhythm. He stopped and held her tightly as the rain bounced off their bodies.

"I love you, Jason," said Shelia. "I will always love you, even if we lose it all."

Jason giggled.

"So I don't have to ask you 21 questions, huh?"

Sheila turned around and sat on the front bumper. Jason's penis throbbed as she held it in her hand. Jason looked down at her and smiled. Sheila smiled back as she looked up at him.

"We rose together, and if it's in the script, we'll fall together." Jason then leaned down and kissed her.

"Now let me finish showing you how much I love you," said Shelia. "Let me taste you."

Jason lay back on the hood of the car as Sheila gave him a taste of heaven, taking in all of his length. Jason's eyes rolled back in his head as Sheila moved faster, twisting her hand as she came up. Jason pulled her hands away and interlocked them with his. Sheila's lips got tighter around his dick as she sucked harder and harder.

Jason couldn't take it anymore as she jerked him up and down, juggling his balls in her mouth. "Baby, I'm 'bout to *come*, oh shit girl. You are too good to me."

Sheila put him back inside her mouth and pumped him furiously, until he exploded. The hot liquid flowed down her throat. Sheila sucked, without missing or letting a drop exit her mouth. Jason laid back and exhaled loudly.

After swallowing all of him, Sheila then lay upon him, and said,

"I never want to be without you, Jason Wright."

The rain mixed with her tears as Jason kissed her eyelids. Sheila started laughing.

"Damn nigga, you get me all emotional. You better not tell anyone that I cry so much."

Jason let his fingertips caress her back as he kissed her forehead.

"You know I don't even talk enough to tell anyone that you are an emotional freak."

Sheila slapped his chest.

"Only you get me that way."

Chapter 22

"Thank you for helping us with this. We just want to get this money and get out of here," said Italy as she, Tanya and Savion pulled into the apartment complex where she and Donavan lived.

Savion remained silent in the backseat.

"Damn, who's worse, you or Jason? Do you talk at all?" Tanya said.

Savion smirked at the comparison of himself with Jason. He thought about how different they were. Jason was well mannered and always seemed serious, while Savion lived for the moment.

"There is nothing to talk about," he said. "Let's just get this over with so I can go about my business. Is dude at home?"

Italy shrugged. "Let me check," she said, dialing the number on Tanya's cell phone.

Donovan picked up the phone on the first ring.

Italy remained silent for a moment.

"Hey baby," she said, disappointed. "I'm on my way home now."

Donovan started yelling as Italy quickly hung up the phone. She hadn't been home or called in three days.

"Damn, he's home. Let's do this another time."

"Hell naw!" Savion shouted. "We're doing this right now!

When you get in there, just put it on him real good and stick to the plan."

Italy put her hand on the side of her face and leaned against the window. She suddenly felt fear rise inside of her, and wished she could just back out and run away, but it was too late. Italy didn't trust Savion, and was scared to death of him. Tanya sensed her worry and interlocked her fingers with Italy's. Italy squeezed tight as she looked ahead of her. Fear, pain and worry was exchanged in the clutches.

Savion watched them and smirked to himself. Knowing they were scared only excited him more. He pulled out his Glock-9 and checked the clip. The street lamps above reflected off the bullets.

"Go in there, Italy. If he starts to trip and starts hitting you, accept it and stick to the script, or run out of there and I'll handle the rest."

Tanya's eyes became humongous.

"We ain't trying to kill nobody!" said Tanya. "That ain't part of the script."

"Well, shit happens, baby. Nothing ever goes how you want it. So, you just sit there and be cute, and drive when I tell you to. Go ahead, Italy, I don't have all day."

"Savion, let's just call Jason. This doesn't feel right, right now."

"Fuck Jason right now! He ain't trying to be a part of this. I'm running this one here, so get off his nuts and do what the fuck I tell you. Don't make me go in there myself."

Italy shook her head and opened the door.

Tanya grabbed her arm.

"You don't have to do shit. Fuck this nigga. We can do it our way."

Italy shut the door as Tanya started the car.

Savion slapped her in the back of the head.

"Turn this damn car off," he said, slapping her again.

Tanya turned the car off.

"No you didn't just hit me, nigga!" she said, turning around in her seat.

Savion put the gun in her face.

"Shut the fuck up! Damn, you got a fucking attitude. First you two were all juiced, and now you sit here scared and shit. You came to me for help. Don't make me do something I don't want to do."

Tanya looked down the barrel of the gun in her face. Savion pushed the weight of the gun against her skull, making her shake within.

Italy looked on in shock.

"Okay, I'm going in. Just put that gun up, please. I'm going in."

Savion mugged Tanya, really wanting to shoot her, as he tucked the gun in his coat.

Storms in hell burned in Tanya's eyes as she wished she had a gun to shoot him right there.

Italy slowly walked to the door. She stood and looked at the double-coated green paint for a second before entering. Donovan sat on the couch with a bottle of Hennessey.

"Hey baby," she said softly as she shut the door behind her.

Donovan took a swig from the bottle and didn't answer. Italy stood against the door, looking at the floor.

"Where you been?" he said after a long silence.

"I had to take some time to myself to think."

"To think, huh? What the fuck you had to think about? What, you thinking about leaving me?"

Italy remained quiet.

Donovan took another gulp of the alcohol, smacked his lips, and put the bottle on the coffee table. He got up and stood in front of Italy. The liquor streamed out of his pores, burning Italy's nose as he leaned into her.

"You been thinking about leaving me?" he said again, grazing her hair.

Italy felt she was staring into the eyes of the devil himself. The humming from the refrigerator took over the room, as Italy shook in fear.

Donovan continued playing with her hair.

"Answer me!" he shouted, making her jump.

Italy suddenly felt weak. She moved without knowing, shaking her head, no.

Donovan let an eerie smile creep across his face.

"Better not, because you know you ain't going nowhere!" he shouted into her ear. His thin frame shook in anger as Italy watched the veins poke out of his neck as he spoke.

Italy felt tears fall from her eyes.

"Why the fuck are you always crying? You're too damn emotional. Wipe your eyes and stop that shit!" he yelled into her ear.

Italy quickly wiped her eyes as Donovan squeezed her breasts hard, while kissing and biting her neck in the same fashion. Italy pulled back, as Donovan forced himself on her. He proceeded with fury and grabbed her thigh, trying to pull it up.

"Don, please stop, baby," Italy said.

Italy pulled all the way off him.

"Don, I need to talk to you. Can we take this slow? I have something to tell you, and I need your help."

Donovan panted hard. The liquor had taken effect. He started seeing double.

"I don't feel like talking. Take your clothes off. I need to fuck you right now."

Italy wrapped her arms around herself.

"I don't want that right now, Don, I-"

Donovan quickly smacked her.

"Shut the fuck up. I don't give a fuck what you want."

Italy held her face as the tears poured.

Donovan stood over her.

"Who you been fucking? You're normally a horny bitch.

Who you been with?"

Before Italy could answer, she was holding her face again. Donovan had punched her in the mouth. All of her strength crept from her body as her face met the floor while Donovan stood over her.

"Who you been with?" he said repeatedly, as he punched her viciously.

Italy screamed as he pulled her by the hair to the kitchen. She kicked and yelled, hoping Tanya would hear her.

"Shut up!" he said, punching her again. "You want to leave me, bitch? After all I've given you? You come in my house with another man's dick on your breath? You disrespect me, *and* got the nerve to scream, bitch? Shut the fuck up," he said, kicking her.

Italy clawed at Donovan's face as she tried to get to her feet. He staggered back as she got up and ran to the door. Donovan shook it off, and ran after her.

Italy quickly grabbed the bottle of Hennessey and threw it at him with all she had in her. The bottle broke against his head, making him scream as the glass and alcohol mixed into the bloody gash now burning on the side of his face. Donovan fell and grabbed his face as Italy ran out the door.

Tanya and Savion saw Italy run out the door and quickly took action. Savion got out of the car, as Donovan came to the door. He pulled his Glock from under a pea coat and pointed it at him.

Donovan stopped in his tracks and turned to run back in the house as Italy got into the car with Tanya. Tanya put the car in reverse and started to pull out.

"No wait!" Italy said, putting her hand on Tanya's.

"Wait for him, Tee. I just got my ass beat bad. Let him do what he has to do."

Tanya put the car in park as they watched.

Savion tripped Donovan as they ran into the house. Donovan fell, scrapping his face on the floor as Savion put the gun to the back of his head.

"Get yo' bitch ass up," he said, pulling him by his t-shirt to his feet. Donovan fell on the stairs, breathing hard and bleeding from the face. Savion stuck the gun into his open mouth.

"Suck it nigga, don't say shit. Point to where the money at."

Donovan didn't move.

"Don't play stupid now, nigga," Savion said. "You had enough energy to beat up ya' bitch, so you have enough to show me where the loot at."

Donovan pointed upstairs as Savion clicked the safety off.

"Show me," he said, pulling Donovan up.

Savion pushed him up the stairs, keeping the gun pointed at his head.

Donovan crawled to the floorboard, panting as if he were taking his last breath.

"Who the fuck are you?" he asked between breaths.

Savion put the gun back in his mouth.

"Nigga, don't ask no fucking questions. You should have known better than to put a ripper where you rest at."

Donovan grew angry as he tried to move towards the stairs.

"Hold up, nigga! Don't be mad now. Yeah, the bitch set you up. The cold part is, I don't even know her or give a fuck about her. That's cold, huh?"

Fire blazed in Donovan's eyes.

Savion pulled the gun out of his mouth and tossed a duffle bag in front of him.

"Fill it up," he said, pulling Donovan's chrome 45 out of the floorboard.

He held one of the guns to his head and the other to the back of his neck as Donovan began filling the bag.

Donovan sniffed the blood back into his nose.

"Since you don't give a fuck about the bitch, take all of

this shit and let me get to her. Let me do that, and just consider this a come up."

Savion thought about it for a moment and laughed.

"Okay, I don't give a fuck. Hurry up and fill that bag up."

Donovan filled the bag up and zipped it. Savion put one of the guns in his waistband and ushered Donovan down the stairs with the other.

"Wait right here. I need a car to get away from here in."

Donovan balled his fists and sat on the stairs, completely sober and full of thunder.

Savion went to the car.

"Get out," he said to the girls.

Tanya and Italy looked up at him in surprise.

"Let me drive. I know how to get to this spot quicker."

Tanya got out of the car and let him in.

Savion quickly pulled his gun out and stuck it in Italy's face.

"Get out! Scandalous ass bitch, trying to get a nigga, well you just got, *got*. Get the fuck out!"

Italy's eyes bulged as Savion opened the door for her. Italy didn't move. "Savion please don't do this. That money is all I have."

Savion laughed.

"You got more than that. Donovan is waiting right inside that door. Get the fuck out, bitch!"

Savion pushed her out of the car as he pulled out of the driveway. He watched her roll to the side as Tanya banged on the window. Savion shut the passenger side door and before he drove off, he stopped the car and rolled the window down.

"Y'all better get out of here. Donovan!" he shouted.

Donovan came storming out of the house.

Savion laughed at the fear that crept across their faces.

"Holla!" he said, laughing as he drove off.

Italy and Tanya took off running after the car as Donovan chased them. The two of them ran like mad women down a semi empty Mission Blvd., screaming at the top of their lungs. Donovan remained close on their heels as they pumped their legs harder and faster while the lights of Tanya's car disappeared. The pain and burn started, but neither could stop. Donovan chased them with all of his might, while cars honked as they ran across traffic.

"Italy, hurry up girl," Tanya yelled, as her track runner thighs pumped across the concrete.

Italy drifted a few feet behind her. Donovan could smell her scent, as he got closer to her. Italy felt like she was going to faint. Her legs became weaker and her heart felt as if it was going to burst through her chest.

A police car cruised by on the other side of the street, but Donovan paid no attention to it. Italy hated the police, but was happy to see them as she started jumping up and down, screaming at the car while they glanced her way. That move slowed her down, and Donovan took full advantage. He balled his fists and hit her in the mouth with all his power.

Italy felt her jaw snap as she hit the pavement. Tanya stopped and began running back to her. The blow made Italy fly back a few feet in the air before hitting the cold hard concrete.

Donovan stood over her, kicking her in every spot on her body. Unsatisfied, he began stomping her head into the pavement.

Italy slowly rolled over, pebbles from the concrete stuck in her face. Donovan saw nothing but red as he continued stomping her head into the hard black gravel.

Italy felt her senses fading from her. Her vision started to slip as her eyes closed, blacking out of the moment. Donovan's evil distorted face was the last thing she saw, as Tanya tried to push and hit him.

Her punches were like butterflies as he grabbed her by the throat and began squeezing. His power raised Tanya on her tiptoes. Donovan punched her in the face, knocking her to the floor as sweat dripped from his face, staining Italy's lifeless body. Timberland boots crunched the gravel beneath him as he approached Tanya, who was trying to scoot back and get to her feet. Donovan grabbed her leg and pulled her to him, while cars began to slow and watch the scene.

Tanya's eyes drifted to Italy as she lay unconscious.

"You killed her, muthafucka," she screamed at him.

"Shut the fuck up, bitch. You want to rob me? You want to send niggas to stick me up? Bitch, I'll kill your trifling ass."

"Freeze" he heard behind him in a deep baritone voice.

Donovan stopped, looked around, and slowly snapped back to reality, as he watched all the cars watching him.

A spotlight glowed behind him.

"Put your hands above your head," the cop said, holding his Glock with both hands.

Donovan realized what he had done. He looked down at Tanya, whose face seemed swollen. With no remorse, Donovan grinned and spit on her.

"Get down on your knees and put your hands behind your head," the cop said, moving closer to him.

Donovan did what he was told, never breaking his stare with Tanya. "They can't hold me forever. You know what's good when I catch you."

Tanya was helped to her feet by a cop, as the other handcuffed Donovan. Tanya began screaming as she ran to Italy's side. Italy didn't move. Tanya kneeled over her, shaking, and not wanting to touch her for fear of hurting her more. One cop pulled her away.

Donovan laughed while the other cop shoved him in the back of the police car.

Tanya looked at him as he grinned in their direction.

"You fucking monster," she screamed, running to the police car.

One of the policemen grabbed her by the waist and held her tightly as she tried to wiggle and kick her way free.

The paramedics showed up and rushed to put Italy into the back of the ambulance. "Sergeant, we have to rush her in now. She may have a fractured skull," a paramedic said.

Tanya collapsed to the ground.

The first police car drove off with Donovan in the back.

"Ma'am stay with us now. Everything is going to be all right. We're going to have to check you for injuries. We also need to ask you some questions as to what caused all of this."

The other cops that had showed up on the scene picked her up and helped her to the police car. Tanya sat in the back and watched the ambulance drive off. She prayed Italy was alive, wishing it was all a dream, and when she woke up, she and Italy would be in her car, drunk and passed out.

"God, I can't lose her. Please don't take my sister," she whispered as they followed the screaming ambulance.

Tanya felt the side of her face, running her fingers over a knot, which had formed next to her right eye. Her butt and thighs were burning from Donovan's dragging as her mind drifted to Savion driving off, laughing in her car. *I'ma kill him and Jason*, she thought. She knew Savion couldn't be trusted. *Jason is involved in this in some kind of way too*, she thought.

"They had to have all of this planned. Sheila's ass too," she whispered.

She thought about what she would tell the police. She knew she couldn't tell them everything, instead, she decided to tell them that they were sitting around drinking and Donovan flipped out.

Tanya decided to report her car stolen. If only she knew Savion's last name. He would have to wait, as she decided not to leave Italy's side until she was back to normal.

Chapter 23

Gooney smiled ear to ear as he listened to the information on the other end of the phone. Karin stood at the stove, mixing a batch of the purest cocaine, with just a pinch of baking soda. Gooney looked out the blinds at the chilly sunny day, typical of California's weather. Karin ear hustled on the conversation as she stirred the coke together. Gooney continued to pace around Karin's apartment, keeping his eyes glued to her movements.

"So you telling me the nigga had a ripper under him and the bitch had some nigga rob him? That's the funniest shit ever. Niggas thought that nigga was the one to have the block on lock? Shit, he deserved to get licked."

Karin stirred harder, as she knew Gooney was talking about Donovan.

Gooney smiled as he realized he was making her upset. Four days prior, Gooney had started to have feelings of love run through his mind for Karin. He decided to follow her one day in one of Malikie's under buckets.

After waiting patiently outside of her job for five hours, Donovan's black Mustang roared into the parking lot and parked directly next to him. Gooney leaned back in the seat and covered his face with his arm as if he was asleep.

Karin sauntered to the car in full bliss. She deep throated Donovan as soon as the car door closed. Donovan threw the car in reverse and sped out of the parking lot. Gooney sat up, shaking his head at what he already knew, so shock was out of the question. Quickly jumping into traffic and following them, Gooney watched as Karin's silhouette bobbed up and down as if she was trying to find an apple under water. With the anger getting deeper and stronger, Gooney felt the want to shoot them both at every stop light.

For the next thirty minutes, Gooney followed Donovan's Mustang through the streets of east Oakland. After lighting a blunt at 79th and Bancroft, he cocked back the hammer on his 45 and sped up to the side of the car. Karin's back was facing him as Donovan continued to navigate through the traffic, seeming not to even care that his dick was being sucked. Gooney smiled as he took one last hit of the blunt and rolled his window down.

Donovan focused on the road as he noticed a grey 87 Nissan Dotson pull up quickly on his right side. Paying it no attention, and continuing to enjoy the head Karin was giving, Donovan didn't notice the chrome barrel hanging out of the window as Gooney sped up with one hand on the heat and the other on the wheel.

The light turned red at 98th street and Bancroft. Gooney stopped smoothly and leaned back into the seat.

Donovan looked around as Karin began to suck with more fury, trying to squeeze the cum out of him.

Looking to his right, Donovan suddenly noticed the barrel of a 45 pointed his way.

Donovan quickly ducked down and hit the gas with all his might, causing the car to fish tail from the light as Gooney let off three shots at the car, busting out the back window. Realizing his car was no match for the muscle of Donovan's speed demon, Gooney tucked the gun under the seat and slowly turned right, headed towards east 14th as he watched Donovan's Mustang disappear. He smiled and hoped that Donovan knew it was him.

"Well at least that nigga is out of the way. I was this close to ending his shit any way the other day. I know he knew it was over for him on that block, but I know that nigga would try to take it back at least one time. Don't nobody know who the nigga was that got him?"

Gooney smiled deeper as Karin slammed the pot into the sink. Frustrated, she turned around and grabbed her purse, trying to head for the door.

"Let me call you back," Gooney said, hanging up his cell phone and grabbing Karin's arm.

"Where you think you going?" he said, yanking her around. "Why you getting all upset? What's that all about?"

"Nothing, Goon, I just really don't feel like being bothered. The rocks are in the freezer chilling. I'm about to go shopping, I need to clear my head."

Gooney let her arm go as he nodded his head. "All that talk about ya' man got you heated, huh?"

Karin stopped in her tracks as Gooney eased behind her.

"Yeah, I know all 'bout that. I know you were sucking that nigga's dick the day I popped off shots at y'all in traffic. I know you been trying to play me for a sucka. But you know what? I'm not even tripping, because that nigga is gone, and I'm the last nigga out here with all the power. That's what your big pussy ass is attracted to. You'll do anything for the nigga with all the money and power. So yeah, I know, but you don't know how much I'm laughing." Gooney said as he grabbed both of her breasts in his hands from behind.

Karin exhaled as her body became relaxed in his arms.

"You knew this whole time?" she whispered, thinking he was on a forgiveness tip.

"Yeah, you forget who you are dealing with. I tried to kill both of you, but you are lucky Donovan's car has some get up," he said as he squeezed harder.

Karin melted like butter as Gooney lifted her skirt and

ripped her thong off. Her pussy jumped as she felt Gooney violently bite her butt as he pushed her head into the wall. She was ready for rough sex, at Gooney's expense.

"We both know how yo' freaky ass love it, bitch," he said as he pulled his sweat pants down and shoved his manhood into her asshole.

Karin jumped as Gooney wrapped his hand over her mouth, muffling her screams as he continued to push his throbbing penis further into her tight orifice.

Karin's body shook as Gooney's head pierced the entry and kept pushing, ripping her skin apart. Trying to shake free was impossible, as he held his hand over her mouth and the other on her waist, controlling his pounding strokes with no regard for her pain.

Gooney shoved deeper and harder into her as he pulled her head back into him. Although she loved the feeling, she now sensed the punishment for her error.

"Bitch, I told yo' dumb ass in the beginning to never cross me. You lucky this is all you're getting so stop squirming and accept it."

Gooney pulled his 10-inch penis out of her, then quickly rammed it back into her, slamming Karin's head harder into the wall. As her juices began flowing, Gooney pumped harder and harder until he climaxed inside her.

Karin whimpered soft cries, scared for her life, as he took his hand off her mouth. Shock and burning pain shot through her body as she slipped to the floor, once Gooney released her. Laughing the whole time, Gooney took the opportunity to release the piss he had been holding all over Karin's limp body.

"I told you not to fuck with me," he said as he let the piss flow freely from his penis, covering her face to her feet.

"You wanted to try and play the game with the game, and now look at you. You are sooo lucky this is all you are getting."

Karin gagged as the fluid got into her mouth. Gooney continued laughing as he kicked her once and spit into her eye.

Karin had never been so humiliated in her life, as Gooney stood over her shaking his dick and holding a pack of cocaine.

"Now, that is all I'm going to do. I want you to get your black ass up now and go get into the shower. Take this to get your mind right and let go of what just happened to you. Now you know not to ever try and play me again," he said, tossing the baggy at her.

Karin wiped her mouth and the spit from her eye. Gooney stood back, watching her as she struggled to get to her feet. Now standing eye to eye, Karin wished she had a gun to shoot him dead in his tracks, but instead, she clutched the baggy of cocaine to her chest as she made her way to the bathroom.

Gooney watched her close the door, and sat down on the couch and turned the TV on ESPN.

Karin peeled her clothes off and stared at herself in the mirror. The smell of urine stained her upper lip and dripped through her hair. Glancing down at the baggy of coke, she quickly snatched it up and poured it over a mirror. Looking through her pocket book, she found a credit card. She chopped it up and evened the powder out. Gooney turned the TV down as he waited patiently for the end.

Karin threw the card to the side and put a finger over her left nostril as she sniffed with the right. Without warning, the powder rushed to her brain and burst like Fourth of July fireworks. She screamed, knocking the mirror off the sink as she fell to the floor. Gooney jumped up and ran to the bathroom to catch her shaking on the floor in convulsions. He knelt down over her and held her head in his hand.

"I bet when you woke up this morning, you never seen this coming, huh? That was a little tiny bit of coke in the bag, but the rest was crushed up glass. Tiny shards of glass straight to yo dumbass head. All I can say, Karin, was that I told you not to play with me. Now here you are."

With the utterance of his last word, Karin's eyes rolled back into her head, as she lay lifeless in his hands. Gooney gently put her head down and closed the bathroom door, and then he calmly walked out of the apartment.

"Jay, this house is the one. I want this house, Jay."

Sheila's diamond ring glittered on her finger as she talked with her hands.

The owner smiled to himself, watching the two of them. The one level, two-car garage home rested in the small city of Tracy.

Jason squinted at the manicured lawn as Sheila ran her hands across his back. Jason looked up and down the street. It seemed the whole area had the same type of homes. Kids of all races played in the street while their parents talked on their porches.

Jason grinned and nodded his head. "Do I make the money order out to you?"

The old man clasped his hands together. His plaid shirt and jeans fit stiffly on his body. His grey hair was cut neatly, and combed back on his head. Deep, dark blue eyes lit up at Jason's question. Towering above the short slim built owner, Jason thought he looked like Mr. Furley from the show, *Three's Company*.

"Mr. Wright, I'm happy to be renting this house to you and your beautiful wife."

Sheila blushed at his statement.

"Thank you!" she said, clinging to Jason.

Jason extended his hand.

"Please, Mr. Anderson, call me Jason. I'm happy you are choosing to rent it to us with no credit check and all."

"Oh Jason, don't worry about it. I like your respect and demeanor. You two remind me of the missus and I when we first got our house. She was just as excited as Sheila is now. All I ask is that you keep up the yard. Mrs. Anderson put a lot of work into this yard. She made me cut it every weekend."

"No problem," Sheila said. "Jason will be doing the same thing because he knows I live for a neat house. How soon can we move in?"

Mr. Anderson reached in his back pocket for his contract papers.

"As soon as you two put your names right here, along with the down payment, the keys are yours."

Jason ran his hand over Sheila's butt.

"Go get a money order."

"Jay, I don't know my way around here. Mr. Anderson, is there a bank around here?"

"Please call me Bobby, and yes, there is a Washington Mutual a few blocks from here. I'll wait here while you two handle your business. Nosey Emma seems to be trying to get my attention."

"Well go on then, Bobby," Sheila smiled at him.

Jason reached over and popped his collar for him.

"Oh my, what was that?" Bobby said laughing.

"That's just something us young people do when we love ourselves."

Bobby laughed.

"We use to jack our slacks and run our hands over our heads, laying our hair down. You learn something new every day. I'm going to enjoy you two."

Chapter 24

"We have to start packing this stuff up tonight," Sheila said, lying in their bed.

Jason was on the floor doing push-ups and crunches. He noticed he was putting on weight again, so he wanted it to come back right.

Sheila flipped through a book of baby names in Swahili. She casually looked down at Jason's wide back. *Damn, this baby is gonna be big*, she thought.

"Jay, did you hear me, baby? The sooner, the better."

Jason finished his set and stood up to sip from his water bottle.

"Yeah, we can do that. Bino said he and Trish would help. I don't know where the hell Sav is. The police must've got his ass again. Did those two girls ever call you?"

"Who Tanya and Italy? No, I haven't heard anything from them. Everything must've gone right. Sav must've talked their fast asses into some freaky shit. It has been a week though. Don't let your brain go into hyper drive like you do."

"I know, baby, but I told Sav and those girls to call you as soon as everything was done. Savion knows better, too."

Sheila knew he was starting to stress over the situation. She sat up on her knees and instructed him to sit down. Slowly, but firmly, Sheila massaged his shoulders.

"Jay, lets push the wedding back until everyone is in a

better position to be there. I know you want your brother there, and I do to. We have all the time in the world, you know? You got your GED, and now that we have that out of the way, are you going to start your book?"

Jason let the power of her hands and her soft words take hold of him. He quickly started to forget about Savion and the girls as Sheila kissed his bald head.

"I have to think about what I'm going to write about, first. I was thinking about writing about relationships, but that has been done too many times. I think I'm going to write about my momma's struggles. I think a lot of black women would respect that. We need to buy a computer, though. I understand about the wedding also. We have a lot going on right now and that would only be another stress, so it can wait for now. I want to be married by the end of the year though. It's April now, so we have at least eight months to get it right."

"Yeah," Sheila said, getting excited about their new life.

"Can you be my sexy secretary?" Jason giggled and leaned back to kiss her.

"You know I'm going to want to play doctor when you start school. I might just fall out and let you bring me back to life."

"Why wait until then? I know how to get all the life out of you and then give it back."

"Mmmm," Jason said, laying her on the bed as they began to kiss passionately.

Jason pulled back and stared at his wife to be. He took her hand and kissed her ring finger.

"You know you still got me open right?" Jason said.

Sheila tugged at his hard penis.

"You better not give this to anybody but me," she said, stroking him.

A bang at the door interrupted their moment. The banging continued until Jason answered the door. His hard on turned limp when he saw Tanya standing at the door with her hands on her hips. Her face had a scar on the right side near her eye.

"Open the fucking door, nigga," she said, staring at Jason through the chain linked door.

Jason unhooked the chain and pulled her into the room.

"Get your damn hands off of me," she said, yanking her arm away.

Jason let her go and closed the door. He turned around with the most menacing stare he could make.

Tanya was suddenly scared to death, but she stood her ground.

"Nigga-"

Jason put his hand up, trying to keep his composure. He pointed to the couch as he brushed past her. He sat in his chair and crossed his legs.

Tanya sat down, balling her fists.

"Where's Sav?"

Jason put his hand up again.

"First of all, don't you ever come to my house yelling and screaming. I don't know you and you don't know me. So you have no right to do that. Second of all, respect my house. My wife and I were trying to rest, and here you come with the bullshit. Now calm yourself and tell me what you want. Where is Italy?"

Tanya's knee bounced up and down rapidly as tears began to form in her eyes.

"She is in the hospital."

Sheila came out of the room.

"What's going on in here?" she asked. "Girl what happened to your face?"

Sheila sat down next to Tanya, examining her scar.

"What happened? Where y'all been?" she asked in worry.

"I have been at the hospital with Italy. She was in a slight coma."

Jason's eyes got big. "Coma? Who put her in a coma?"

"Donovan! Savion played us. Donovan beat the shit out of her and fractured her skull. He stomped her head in the ground. Savion took my car, but they found it in Oakland."

"Is Italy still out?" Jason asked, knowing that something like this would happen.

"No, she woke up a few days ago. She's in so much pain. Why did y'all do us like that?" Tanya pleaded in tears.

"We didn't do anything to you, girl. You can cut that right now," Sheila calmly spoke. "Jason told you that the situation was not cool, but you chose to do it anyway."

Jason looked to the floor in silence. He wondered where Savion was and what caused him to snap.

"Let's go to the hospital," he said, thinking of Italy.

Sheila looked at him in surprise. Her eyes followed him as he walked to the room to get a shirt.

Tanya sat in tears.

"Where is Savion at, Sheila? I want to kill that nigga. He played us real bad. You don't know where he is?"

Sheila shook her head.

"The last time we heard from him was the night he left with y'all. Here we go again with this nigga. I'm sick of this fool. Me and Jason don't even get down like that. I told Jay this would happen. Now he's going to spend his time stressing on that fool. We're moving into our home within the next few days. I don't need this shit."

The jealous side of Sheila was emerging as she wondered why Jason wanted to go to the hospital to see Italy.

Jason came out of the room with his keys in hand.

"Sheila, put your shoes on. Let's go!"

Chapter 25

"Damn, you look like shit," Jason whispered into Italy's ear.

Sheila eyed him suspiciously. Italy's face was still bruised, with stitches over her left eye. She also had two black eyes from having her nose broken. The top of her head was wrapped in bandages as she blinked her eyes open, cutting them at Jason. Her lips forced a smile, which also had six stitches. Jason noticed it and held her hand in his.

"Don't smile, it looks like it hurts."

"It does," she said in a barely audible tone. "Where's Tanya?"

"She went to get some orange juice. We just wanted to come and see how you are doing. We just found out what went down. I truly am sorry."

Italy struggled to sit up.

"Jason, you didn't know what was going to happen, did you?"

Jason shook his head.

Italy smiled and looked over at Sheila, who was shooting daggers at her. "Hey Sheila, did y'all get married yet?"

Sheila's frown broke into a smile as she grabbed Jason's arm.

"No, not yet. We are going to wait until everyone can attend, and all the BS settles down. I did get my ring, though."

Italy struggled to sit up and glance over at Sheila's extended hand.

"That's phat, girl. You have real class. Jay, where's Savion? Did he come to your spot after what happened?"

Jason tensed, thinking about Savion.

"I haven't seen him at all. I'm going to find him, though. Don't worry about it."

Italy looked at the ceiling.

"You told me, huh? That's the one thing that has been going through my head since I woke up."

"Don't worry about it. It has happened. The thing is, not to let it happen again. Is anyone looking out for you besides Tanya?"

Italy rolled her eyes, thinking about Beth.

"Tanya's enough. Damn I need a joint. Y'all have some weed with you?"

Sheila shook her head, laughing. "No, but I have you covered when you get home. We're moving within the next few days, so we'll come back through."

Italy looked disappointed as Jason stared down at her, caressing her hand.

The feeling of being cared for made Italy smile.

"Where are y'all moving to?"

"We got a house out in Tracy. You and Tanya have to come through when you get better," Jason said, feeling around her stitches.

"Damn, he beat you up real bad, huh?" Sheila said, letting her frown return.

Jason sensed her jealousy.

"Sheila, wait for me outside, please. Let me have a few minutes alone with Italy."

Sheila smacked her lips and stood back. Jason arched his eyebrows at her. Sheila bit her bottom lip to keep from saying something foul. She had never seen Jason treat any other woman with care, except her and his mother. Sheila stormed out of the room while Jason watched the door close, shaking his head.

"She seemed pretty mad, Jay. Maybe you should go."

Jason pulled up a chair next to her bed.

"Don't worry about Sheila. She's never seen me care about any other chick except her."

"So you care, now? I thought you didn't give a fuck."

"And I thought you were smarter than you looked. When are you going to listen for a change?"

Italy let out a low soft breath while looking at the ceiling.

"Jason, a lecture is something I really don't need right now. I'm thinking about where I'm going to live when I get out of here. I have to steadily watch my back now, since Savion fucked us. I have no money, and a bunch of clothes. You aren't trying to help me, so save it. Things are hard enough without you telling me how much of a wreck I am. Okay!" Italy's words were barely audible.

Jason retained his composure.

"Where are your parents?"

Italy sat silent while she and Beth's last conversation played in her head. "Jason, please leave. I'm sleepy and I really don't feel like opening closed doors. Just leave!"

Jason pursed his lips and shook his head. He stood up over Italy without saying a word. Italy met his eyes as Jason saw all the pain and worry in her glance. He knew she was seeking help, but her trust in anyone except Tanya didn't exist. Jason caressed her hand again and walked out. He heard her whisper, "Thank you" as the door closed.

Sheila and Tanya sat on a blue bench in the hallway. The hospital reeked of sickness and disinfectant. A man holding his bleeding head rested on a gurney next to them. The girls stood up when they saw Jason calmly walk out of the room. Sheila gave off an uncomfortable vibe.

"Is she all right?" Tanya asked, taking the seal off the orange juice.

Her tired face showed nervousness; dark rings and bags had started to form under her eyes as she bore no makeup and desperately needed a re-braid.

"Yeah, she's fine," he said. "Tanya, where is Italy going to sleep when she gets out of here? What's the deal with her parents?"

Tanya put one hand on her hip, while tapping her foot on the floor. She liked the way Jason acted as if he cared, but still thought he knew more than he was giving off.

"Why, Jason? Are you going to put her up? Don't worry about..."

"Damn, shut your fucking mouth for one minute! I told you your attitude will get you fucked up. I didn't do this to y'all. I told you to leave it alone. Be mad at yourselves. Now I'm sorry about what happened to you, but I'll be damned if I accept your attitude. What the hell is wrong with y'all? Italy just copped an attitude also, and all I'm trying to do is make sure she will be all right after this. Forgive me for giving a fuck. You know what? It's my bad for even dealing with y'all. I hope you two get it together. Get her some good books to read. She's not doing anything else!"

Jason turned his back, and walked quickly to the front doors, followed by Sheila.

Tanya watched them walk through the doors before going into Italy's room.

Chapter 26

Donovan paced back and forth in the small Santa Rita cell, thinking about the last taste of freedom that he had just a mere two weeks ago. Santa Rita, the east Bay's main county jail served as a reception center for inmates headed back to prison or going through court trials for pending time. Oakland, Hayward and San Leandro suspects mainly filled up the prison like buildings, often going crazy from the confinement.

Donovan listened to the howling of other inmates slowly losing every ounce of sense they once had, or inmates talking to others through the thick metal doors, holding in all the rage the heart of struggle can muster.

Pacing continuously, Donovan kept replaying the last free night, and the look on Italy's face as she lay on the cold concrete. Half of her face was smothered into the pebbles as his foot stomped out the thin level of life left in her eyes. Smiling, he stopped at the small window carved into the metal door and looked out into the dark hallway, searching for any sign of life.

After seeing nothing, and turning around to face the empty companionship of the cold cell, Donovan took off his county issued blue jumpsuit and began doing push-ups. The moon light lit his body in the late hours as he became more enraged with every up and down motion.

"You know it's town bizness, nigga," someone yelled out

of their cell to another.

Donovan stood up and looked out the window, barred and stained from years of others before him. Shaking his head, he slid down to the floor for another set.

I'ma kill the bitch soon as I touch, he thought to himself. She had to be out of her fucking mind to try to take anything from me.

Keys jingled at his door as he went down for the fortieth push up. He quickly stood up and got into a fighter's stance, in case this was a CO, wanting to release some anger. Donovan watched anxiously for the door to open, possibly to get off the first swing.

"What you doing, nigga? You thought I was coming in here to whup you?"

"Can never be too sure, you know how these crackers are. What you up to, Brenda?"

Brenda was another old flame from around the way that Donovan used to mingle with. Brenda loved the rough way Donovan would fuck her, compared to her loving white husband. Giving up hoeing for a more proper life as a CO, Brenda sometimes missed the streets, and often relived her heydays by fucking the old gangsters who had put it on her the best. Tonight was no different, but there were more important matters at hand.

"Oh nothing! I heard you were down here and I just came to holler at you and see if you needed anything. You know I still love yo' ass, nigga."

"Is that right? Anyway, you still married?"

Brenda flashed her ring at him as he sat down on the bunk.

"That's what's up. Yo', I need you to do me a huge favor. I need you to get in touch with Karin for me. I can't remember her number for the life of me. It is in my phone at my crib. The keys should be in my belongings they holding up there. You remember Karin, right?"

Brenda shook her head as she looked back at the main podium.

"Yeah, I remember her ass. Or shall I say I remembered her. You ain't heard what happened?"

Donovan looked up with a questioning expression.

"Naw, what happened?"

"Karin is dead, baby. They found her in her apartment like two days ago. The neighbor said she smelled a foul smell coming from her spot. The manager went in there and found her naked on the floor, dead from an overdose they say, but they also said they suspect foul play."

Donovan closed his eyes and put his face in his hands. For seconds, he felt what seemed to be tears well up in his eyes, but quickly dismissed them and replaced the feeling with rage at the thought of Gooney.

Brenda smacked her thick lips as she swayed her thick chocolate frame to his side. The long weave she sported covered the top of his head as she bent over to give him a hug.

"Don't even trip, baby. You know how the game goes. She was probably getting down foul with somebody and the game checked her for it."

Donovan sat in silence, knowing he was the reason Karin was now dead. Finally, in death, he realized that Karin loved him and was willing to do anything for him.

Donovan shrugged off Brenda's hug and stood up to gather his thoughts. Brenda put her hands on the tight fitting uniform, showing off all of her voluptuous curves as Donovan stood at the window. Dismissing the thought of sex with this rugged man, Brenda backed out towards the door.

"Well, I got to get back to work, baby. You know if you need anything, don't be afraid to holler. I work the night shift Monday through Friday."

Donovan nodded as Brenda closed the door and locked it as she stared at him through the small window.

What the fuck is going on? Donovan thought to himself.

How this nigga got me losing everything? I got to bail the fuck out of here and get this shit right. It's no fucking way I'ma let a weak ass nigga and a bitch have me losing.

"Another birthday, huh, Ma? I'm here again. Sorry the presents haven't changed. Fiends even steal from the dead. Things haven't been cool at all. I haven't seen Savion in four months. I don't think he's locked up again. He would've called. Maybe he's sitting next to you up there, finally at peace. My personal life is good. Sheila's stomach is bulging. We've been living in Tracy and doing well."

Jayson wiped his jaw and continued talking to his angel.

"I have a job at the sanitation company. Yes, I'm a garbage man. It was a blow to my ego at first, but my partner is cool, and the pay and benefits are good. Sheila's still in nursing school. I never realized how much drive she has until recently. Here she is about to bust, but she runs the house and flies through school like it's nothing. She reminds me a lot of you. I wonder how things would be if you were still alive. I guess I can only keep living and do the things you taught me."

Jason stood at his mother's grave at the Rolling Hills Cemetery in Oakland. Today was her birthday, and as always, Jason was there with three red roses. The sun beamed bright as he looked over the neatly cut grass and the countless gravesites. Letting out a long, deep breath and looking into the sky, Jason swallowed as he thought about all the love he had lost over the years.

"Damn, you're getting fat, nigga," Savion said, standing next to Jason, looking at his mother's grave.

Jason shot him a quick glance and looked over the hills again.

Savion looked back, and smiled as Jason stared hard at the bright gold shine coming from his mouth.

"I knew you would be out here. Damn, Momma would've been forty-one today," Savion said bending down to put a dozen roses by her grave. "This is the first time I've been out here." He leaned in closer to read the inscription on her grave. 'Always Loved and Remembered'. This picture is phat. You did a good job. How you been, Jay?"

Jason stared down at him without answering.

Savion caught the vibe and continued looking at the gravestone.

"I went by the apartment a couple weeks ago, but your neighbor said you had moved. Where are you staying at now?"

"Tracy," Jason whispered.

Savion kissed the gravestone and stood up, eye to eye, with his brother. Both stood in silence, each wondering what to do next. Savion sucked his teeth and started giggling as Jason continued looking at him in silence. Savion put his arms around him and hugged tight while Jason's body became stiff.

Savion pulled back and held Jason by the shoulders.

"Jay, what's up, man? Why are you tripping?"

Jason shook his head as he put the flowers down and kissed the gravestone.

"I'll be back soon, Momma."

Savion stood, upset as he watched Jason walk away.

"Jason!" he yelled after him.

Jason continued until he reached his car. He noticed a champagne colored Navigator parked behind him. A light-skinned female with long hair sat in the passenger side. Jason darted his eyes at her for a second and got into his car.

Savion caught up and knocked on the window before he could drive off. "Jason? Jay, roll the damn window down."

Jason gripped his steering wheel tightly before lowering the window.

Savion could see his clenched jawbone.

"Jay, why are you acting like a bitch? Nigga, I'm alive and doing way cool. What? You tripping off those two chicken heads? Speak nigga!"

Jason looked up at his brother's steaming, almost red face.

"Everett and Jones. I have to get some BBQ for Sheila. Follow me and we can talk when we get there."

Savion's face smoothed out.

"Let's go," he said, walking back to his Navigator.

Jason and Savion sat on the hood of Jason's car as they waited for their orders.

"Damn, I almost forgot how much I loved the town. I wish I could come back."

Jason lit a Newport and looked at the girl in the truck.

"Who's the chick?"

Savion smiled as he looked at her bobbing her head to the music.

"That's Keisha. I knocked her a few months ago. She lives next door to me. She's fly, huh?"

Jason nodded his head, letting the smoke flow from his nostrils.

"Where are you living at?"

"Fresno," Savion said, rising to his feet.

"Fresno? What the hell is down there?"

"Shit… don't let these small towns fool you. They got money down there. I'm sitting real cool. I used all that money and tripled it. This country cat I know opened his arms and embraced me."

For a few minutes, they sat in a stale silence. Savion became irritated. "Jay, if you gone be an emotional nigga this whole conversation, I'll holler. What's your damn problem?"

Jason flicked his cigarette and stood to face Savion.

"My problem? Nigga you're my damn problem. Why can't you ever just do things the way they are planned? I constantly stick my damn neck out for you, and you add a different cut to it every time."

Savion started to laugh.

"Is that what this is all about? Man, fuck those little

bitches. What if that was you in that position? What if it was Sheila trying to off you for some bread? You should be thanking me. I knew you would have something to say. That's why I haven't been around. You're too fucking soft, Jay. You're scared to look death in the eyes. That's why you always do things the way you do. All in the name of respecting the game, right? Please! That's just an excuse you use because you live in fear. Your bitch has more nuts than you, nigga."

Jason felt the heat of hell burn through his Nikes. Savion knew he had pressed a button. Jason bit the inside of his cheeks as he balled his fists inside his leather coat.

"Y'all order is ready," the short dark skinned waitress said as she went back into the restaurant.

"Thank you," Jason said, with a smile.

Savion started to walk towards the door when Jason grabbed him by the arm.

"I'm going to say this one time, so you'd want to listen. I'm not afraid of anything walking this earth breathing. This isn't about Italy or Tanya. This is about you. You steal some money from a couple of females and now you think you can talk to me any kind of way? Nigga, you weren't talking that shit when I made sure you didn't want for anything in the pen, when I took care of Momma before she died. When I constantly look out for you and worry about your punk ass to the point I can't sleep.

"You want to talk about scared? Muthafucka, I watched both of my parents die. Your mother is the closest you'll get to God, and I watched her die. I live with the pain she went through, the constant tears and the look of defeat and regret in her eyes. I witnessed it! I live with it! And you dare talk down on me? You stay going in and out of jail. You stay getting shot at, robbed, and you talk down on me? Do you know what you are? You are a *"in the way"* ass nigga. That's what you are. The game ain't what it used to be, Sav. Just because I don't run around like I'm Scarface does not, and I repeat, does not mean I'm scared. It's called being smart. It's called having a motive in this business, and that motive is to get money. That's it. You can have all the rest of it because it will be the death of you. I'll still be living. The last one breathing, raising my seed with my wife, breathing.

"You must be a retarded nigga because nobody in their right mind wants to have beef. You think you aren't confused and that's the most dangerous part. You didn't have any foul words to say to me after you got fucked in the ass. No, you ran to me. And you talk down on me? You get a little money and a cute chick and now you're too big for your damn pants. You're ridiculous. Disappear again, nigga."

Savion's smile appeared quickly. He began clapping as Jason stood motionless watching him.

"The almighty Jason has struck back. Maybe your heart doesn't pump Kool-Aid after all."

Jason spit on the ground near Savion's shoes as he turned to walk in the restaurant.

"Don't you turn your fucking back on me, Jay," Savion said, yanking him around.

"I don't need you, nigga. That's why I did what I did, because I'm sick of needing you. Sick of everybody with that 'what did Jason say?' shit. Fuck you and anything you have to say. And if I ever hear you speak on what happened to me, I'm going to kill you, Jay. Do you hear me? Don't push it."

Jason's eyes turned to stone.

"Is that right? You want to kill me? Let's not waste any time with it. How did it feel nigga? How did it feel to have your ass ripped apart then have to run to me? You want to kill me? Do it now. You better do it now. I can find you with no problem, but you know you won't be able to find me. What's it gonna be, Sav?" Jason let his face smooth out as Savion stared quietly.

Savion desperately wanted to shoot him right there, but knew he couldn't pull himself to do it. Jason was his brother, regardless.

Savion bit his bottom lip while nodding his head.

"I'll see you, Jay," he said, walking backwards to his truck.

Jason hated that he had to say the things he'd said, but he felt Savion needed a reality check. Jason stood motionless as his jaw relaxed, watching the Navigator pull away before he walked into the restaurant.

Chapter 27

Italy stood in her mother's kitchen, cooking breakfast. The sun wasn't up yet, allowing the night to collect the entire still of the morning. She put in her Tweet CD, the music slowly blended with the night as she twisted her body to the music. Finally feeling at peace, she thought about the last few months of her life. Beth had allowed her to move in again as she struggled to gather the pieces of her life. Fully recovered from the beating, the occasional migraine slid in every now and then.

"Oooops! There goes my shirt, up over my head. Oh my!" she sang along to the music while scrambling eggs and flipping over sausage patties. She turned the fire down and stood back, gyrating to the music. Her silk slip rose above her thighs as she grinded slowly to the floor, nipples hard as the silk material moved back and forth over her breasts.

Italy turned around to see Bobby, her mother's common law husband, watching her every move. His hand was stuck in his shorts, stroking himself as his hazel eyes ran all over her body. Italy stopped what she was doing and grabbed her robe from the kitchen table.

"What're you looking at?" she said in disgust.

Bobby ran his hand over his balding curly head. His protruding stomach hung over his shorts.

"You're going to learn how to say good morning," he said,

brushing past her.

Italy turned the stereo off and tightened the strap around her waist. Bobby's eyes rested on her butt as she bent down in the refrigerator.

"Damn girl, you getting thick back here," he said, rubbing his hand over her backside.

Italy jumped up and turned around quickly.

"Muthafucka, don't you ever touch me again. Try it and I'll hurt you, Bobby. I ain't playing!"

Bobby started laughing.

"What you gone do? Tell your mama? She isn't going to do anything. I pay the bills here. She'll kick your ass out before going against me."

Italy bowed her head to the floor. She knew he was right. Beth wouldn't care where she went, but she would have to leave there.

"That's better," he said, pulling at the straps of her robe.

Italy slapped his hands away and pulled back.

"Fuck it, then. Let's see what she'll really do," she said, pushing him in the chest.

Bobby barely moved from the light shove, and tried to grab at her robe again. Italy slapped him in the face and tried to push him down.

"Keep your fucking hands off of me. I don't care if this is your house. Don't you ever touch me again."

Bobby started laughing as Italy held her finger out at him.

"Well, it's time for you to get out. I don't care where you go, but you have to get out of here. Go and pack your stuff again. I want you out by 7:00 p.m."

Italy began to tremble.

Beth's footsteps could be heard coming towards them.

"What's going on in here?" she said, coming into the room yawning.

Bobby poured himself a cup of coffee as Beth hugged him from behind.

"Italy doesn't have any respect for anyone. She has to get out of here. I asked her to do one thing, and she catches an attitude with me. I'm not accepting that, Beth. She's got to go."

"He's lying, Momma. He wanted some pussy and I wouldn't, so now he's throwing me out. Make his ass get out!"

Beth lit a cigarette as she stood in front of Bobby, tapping her foot on the floor.

"She's lying, baby. How many times have we been through this shit with Italy? She always says something or does something out of this world. I accepted her back in, because of what happened to her, but now she's back to normal and can get around. She's got to go!"

Beth looked at Italy as she inhaled her cigarette. She scratched her head as Italy waited for her response. Disappointment crossed Italy's face as Bobby kissed Beth on the cheek and walked out the room. Italy shot eye daggers at his wrinkled Indian face as he smiled at her. She couldn't believe the power he had over her mother.

"I don't need to hear this shit right now," Beth said, sitting in a chair at the kitchen table.

"Momma, I know you aren't going to believe him? You know how Bobby is. This isn't the first time he has got at me like this either. He's always trying to get into me."

Beth snapped her head at Italy. She could see the rage on her mother's face and knew what was coming. Beth jumped up from the table and stood eye to eye with her.

"So you been fucking my husband? I knew your little tramp ass wouldn't be worth the pussy you sit on. Get your shit and get out!"

Italy stood in shock.

"Momma, I haven't done anything with Bobby. I can't believe you're putting a man over your daughter. Look at me, Momma. I swear to you. Believe me for a change. Quit putting everyone over me. Think about me."

Beth stood silent as her eyes pierced through Italy. She felt confused about what to do, and the look in Italy's eyes was truthful. Beth began to cry as her cigarette fell to the floor. She collapsed in Italy's arms and held her tightly. Italy wrapped her arms around her mother as she felt the tears flow from her eyes.

"I'm sorry, baby," Beth sobbed. "I'm sorry for not being the mother you need."

"It's okay, Momma," Italy said, pulling her closer.

This was what she missed most about her mother. A simple hug shattered every bit of hate or anger she had for her.

"No, it's not okay, Italy, because you have to leave."

Italy became numb. It felt as if her body wasn't there and the words spoken to her were foreign.

"I believe you, sweetheart, but Bobby pays for everything here. I can't have him leave and both of us out on the street. What good would that do?"

Italy let her arms fall to the side as she closed her eyes to everything. Beth continued to hold her until Italy pulled back. Beth let go and looked at her daughter with sorrow. She saw her child; her five-year-old baby's face and had to fight from breaking down.

Italy opened her eyes to her mother's stare. Beth let her eyes fall to the floor as she tightened her robe. Italy wrapped her arms around herself as she sat down in a kitchen chair. She began to rock back and forth slowly, feeling as if she was losing her mind.

Beth stole a few more seconds of silence before grabbing her cigarettes and walking out of the room.

Italy waited until she heard her mother's bedroom door close, before letting everything she'd been holding in come pouring out of her eyes.

Chapter 28

"Tanya, this is Italy. My mom kicked me out again. I don't know where I'm going to stay. Call me when you get this message."

Italy hung up her cell phone and looked at her bags piled high in a booth in Taco Bell's lobby. She put one hand on her hip and the other on her head as she thought about what she would do next.

A dark blue Yukon pulled into the parking lot with Messy Marv's "Playing with my Nose" thumping loudly, making the windows of the restaurant vibrate. Italy looked at the truck in awe. The chrome Lexani rims almost hypnotized her as she watched the TVs playing inside.

Three girls got out the back as another got out of the passenger side. Italy recognized the girl getting out of the passenger side.

"Bianca," Italy yelled out.

The girl stopped and looked back. Italy waved as she walked towards them. The other girls shot envious stares as the man getting out of the driver's side looked her over. Italy noticed it all, but dismissed the hate.

"Italy, girl what's up? Where have you been?" Bianca said, wrapping her arms around her.

Italy held her for a second, eyeing her entourage. The man continued to eye-fondle her.

"Bee, holler at her," he said, before walking in the restaurant with the other girls.

"What's he talking about?" Italy said, releasing her embrace.

"Nothing girl, don't worry about it. How have you been doing? Last time I heard about you, some nigga had damn near killed you."

"Yeah," she said, squinting from the bright California sun and thought of Donovan.

"Let's go inside, girl. It's hella hot out here." Bianca said, running her eyes over Italy's outfit.

Italy, in return, jocked Bianca's wardrobe. She thought about the last time she had seen her, in hand me down clothes and wild out of control hair.

"Damn Bee, look at you! Shit has changed, huh? What are those, Gucci shoes?"

"Yeah! They're fly, huh? El makes sure we stay fitted."

Bianca moved a strand of hair from her face with a freshly manicured French tipped nail. Her caramel skin was soft and flawless. A pair of Gucci shades blocked her emerald green eyes as her thick thighs were stuffed inside a Gucci skirt, showing off powerful track-walking calves.

"What're you doing out here? Are you waiting for someone?"

"No," Italy whispered. "My mom just kicked me out. I'm waiting for Tanya to call me back, so I can figure out what the hell I'm going to do."

Bianca looked at all the bags of clothes piled into the booth. "Are those all of your clothes?"

Italy nodded her head.

"Well you want to roll with us until Tanya calls you back?"

Italy thought about it for a minute.

"Naw, I'm cool. I'm going to wait here."

Bianca smacked her lips.

"Girl, come on. We just gone chop it up and smoke some

purp."

Italy exhaled.

"El won't trip? Those other girls were mugging the hell out of me."

"That's because they know El thinks you're sexy. You saw the way he was looking at you."

Italy became confused.

"That ain't your man?"

"Yeah, but I don't trip off of him messing with other chicks. It's his job.

"His job?" Italy said, surprised.

"Yeah his job! I'll explain everything to you tonight."

Italy agreed, and they walked to where the group was standing. Bianca introduced her.

"Everybody, this is Italy."

El smiled, revealing a mouth full of platinum diamond teeth.

"What's up, girl? You feel all right?"

"Yeah, I'm okay," she said, under her breath. The other three girls looked her up and down.

Italy looked back at them, trying to show no fear.

Bianca noticed the awkwardness.

"Y'all stop eye-fucking my girl like that. Nobody is thinking of the three of you. El, Italy just got put out of her spot. Can she roll with us for a minute until her friend calls her back?"

"Yeah," El said. "I ain't tripping. Are you hungry?"

Italy shook her head as El stared at her.

"Look baby, you're gonna have to speak up if you are going to kick it with me. Be yourself. We ain't gon' bite you."

Italy managed to crack a smile.

"Naw, she just prissy as fuck," one of the girls shouted.

Italy darted her eyes at the overly thick dark skinned girl. Her short hair was parted and slicked to the side. She was wearing a Los Angeles Lakers jersey dress and Cesare Paciotti sandals. A tattoo of a panther covered her right arm, and she had a pretty face showing a lot of wear and tear. The very thin light-skinned girl cut her hazel eyes at Italy, smacking her thin lips. Italy rolled her eyes, knowing the girl was not that attractive. She barely had any breasts, and too thin hips. Italy knew the backside was just as bad. The last was a very sexy Puerto Rican girl. She was a 10, if Italy had ever seen one. Her long wavy hair hung down to the middle of her back and her lips were full and thick.

"Don't pay these two no mind," she said, extending her hand. "I'm Charlotte."

Italy took her hand. She was thick and bow legged in a pair of Miss Sixty jeans with Donna Karan ankle boots. Italy could almost smell the leather from her jacket.

El broke up the tension.

"Y'all get this food while I help this girl with her bags. C'mon, Italy." El said, walking to the door with bags in hand.

"So, what you get put out for?" he said as he opened the back of the truck.

Italy put her bag in.

"My mom was just tripping. I didn't do anything. She just has issues."

"Do you have a place to go?"

"I don't know yet. That's why I'm waiting for my girl to call me back."

El leaned against the truck and looked her up and down.

"Why do you keep looking at me like that?" Italy said, folding her arms over her chest.

"You're sexy as hell, girl. I can't help myself. Your legs are nice."

Italy blushed at his statement. She did think he was handsome. He was a little too short for her, but still cute. His dark skin was smooth, causing her to reminisce on Jason. His terry cloth Jumpman sweat suit was baggy over his matching Jordans as he lay against the truck, smiling.

"Well get on in the front, so I can talk to you."

Italy got into the truck and looked at all the accessories.

"This is phat. I like the TVs." She said as the rest of the girls piled in.

"Well, maybe we can work on getting you one of these," El said. "You're already worth a million dollars, and judging from the looks of things, you don't even know it."

Italy shifted in her seat as the rest of the girls laughed at the Austin Powers movie playing on the TVs.

"What do you mean?"

El rolled his eyes as he took a sip of his soda.

"Come on, baby. Don't get stupid on me. There is no reason any woman should be broke. Do you know you have what starts wars right between your thighs? Look at you waiting at a Taco Bell with garbage bags full of clothes. You're fine as hell, with no car or no place to lay that pretty head. That ain't living. But going through life with no limits, now that's living. You see us in this truck? We never stress or have a dull moment. We're never angry. Why? We set our own rules.

"What other 19 or 20 year old girls you see draped in all this stuff you can't pronounce-besides NBA niggas' bitches, of course. Singers, yeah, but regular bitches, no. You don't see that too often. But I bet you'll see these four with all that and more. Why? Because sex sells. Men will trick off their paychecks and rent money just to see a beautiful woman. You are beyond beautiful. So just think about how you'd be living if you shake that moral complex. All of this and more would be yours. Bianca is paid, and you're way finer than her."

"Fuck you, El," Bianca yelled from the back seat. "Spit at her, but don't blow her head up with bullshit, because we all know who the baddest bitch is."

Everyone laughed as El pulled the truck onto the freeway.

"So you're a pimp?" Italy said, watching him drive.

El chuckled to himself.

"Pimp is an overrated word. I'm more of a guidance

counselor. Money manager is a better word for it. Pimps have all the control. I leave y'all in control, with a nightly quota. I encourage and push y'all to get the most doe you can, because it fattens your pockets and makes my cut nice. Ya' dig?"

Bianca split a Philly in half and filled it with weed. She sprinkled a few dabs of cocaine down the middle and quickly rolled it up, smiling as she passed the blunt to Italy.

"Light that up and get ya' mind right, girl."

Italy pulled her lighter out of her purse and lit the blunt. El watched her from the corners of his eyes as Italy hit the blunt hard and laid her head back in the seat.

"This tastes kind of funny. What kind of weed is this?"

Bianca leaned forward.

"That's some new shit out the town. It's getting your mind right though, huh?"

Italy nodded her head, passing the blunt to El.

"No, no, sweetie, I don't drink or smoke. Go ahead and enjoy yourself. Let me worry about our finances."

Italy took a few more pulls from the blunt and passed it to Bianca. The other three girls whispered under their breaths as they giggled about how easily she'd been hooked. El caught their eyes in the mirror and gave them his coldest look, stopping all laughter.

A few minutes later, El pulled into the driveway of a single story house. "This is the spot. Let's go inside and chill."

Italy felt on top of the world. She started giggling, feeling as if she was walking on air, while El grabbed her bags and put them in the house.

Bianca put her arm inside of Italy's.

"How do you feel, girl?"

Italy couldn't stop laughing.

"I feel hella good. Thanks girl, I really needed that. That is the bombest weed I've ever smoked. Y'all are doing it big."

"So, do you like El?"

Italy calmed down.

"Yeah, he's cool. I like his thinking. He's smart."

"Girl, you just don't know. When I met him, I was going through it. I was still broke as fuck. My momma had kicked me out too. He came to my rescue, and you see me now."

"All of y'all stay here?"

"Me and Trina do. She's the dark one. Charlotte and Sophia have their own spots in Oakland and Berkeley."

The moon started to rise as the bay winds started to kick in. Italy sat on the leather couch with El, as the rest of the girls cracked open bottles of Hennessey XO and Grey Goose vodka.

"Do you want something to drink?" El asked, opening up a laptop computer on the coffee table.

"You don't mind?" she said.

"That's what it's there for," he said, running his hands through his braids.

Bianca brought her a glass of vodka.

"Drink this. It will warm you up."

Italy took the glass and sipped it slowly. The alcohol burned going down her throat.

"Take it slow, baby. I don't like a lush. I need you clear enough to focus. A drunk bitch forgets to get her doe." El said as he began typing.

Italy giggled.

"What're you doing?" she said, trying to focus her eyes on the computer screen.

"Getting money is easy. Keeping it is the hard part. I'm checking my investments."

"What have you invested in?"

El side eyed her.

"What're you writing a book? You ask a lot of questions."

Italy became quiet.

"I just like to learn about new things, that's all. Is that a problem?"

El smiled.

"No, it is not a problem, but you should be thinking about what you are going to do. Your friend hasn't called you back, and it's getting late. The girls are getting ready to go to work. What're you going to do? This isn't a rest haven. Make up your mind."

Italy took another sip of her drink. The coke laced blunt and the alcohol distorted her thinking as she watched the other girls pop ecstasy pills.

"Italy? Do you want one of these?" Charlotte asked.

"No, she's had enough," El cut in.

Charlotte shook her head.

"I'll tell you what," El continued. "Go out with the girls tonight and see how everything goes. Make your mind up then. Are you down with that?"

Italy nodded.

"Whew! I'm ready to fuck," Sophia said out of nowhere, taking her clothes off.

Charlotte slapped her on her flat yellow butt.

"Girl, you're gaining a little weight."

Sophia laughed. "I know. I've been swallowing."

Bianca put on a glittering thong and bra.

"What's up over here? Italy, are you gone roll with us tonight?"

"Yeah," she said, standing up. "I have a cute Victoria's Secret set to wear."

Bianca laughed.

"That's cool because you won't have it on for long. This party tonight is full nudity. Are you shaved?"

Italy stretched.

"Yeah, but I just need to take a shower. El, do you want to join me?" Everyone stopped what they were doing, anticipating his response.

El didn't look up from his computer.

"I don't mix business with pleasure. Now go get ready, Bitch."

Italy became defensive.

"Bitch? Who are you calling a bitch?"

El put the laptop down and leaned back on the couch.

"You better get used to it, because you are going to be called worse than that. What do you think yall doing out there? Singing Christmas carols? Bitch, hoe, ripper, bop....... Get ready to get called all of those. And one more thing. Don't you ever raise your voice with me again. Nobody here catches attitudes with me. Do you hear me? I've never had to put my hands on a bitch and I don't plan on doing so. As long as you pop that pussy and get this money we are good. This ain't no rest haven at all. Do you hear me?"

Italy nodded her head at his stern voice and serious stare.

"So what's it gonna be, bitch? You ready?" El said not wasting any time.

Again, Italy nodded her head seeming to be paralyzed by his words.

"Hurry up and get ready then, bitch. Time is money," he said before returning to the laptop in front of him.

Chapter 29

Tyrell Ave. was booming as usual. The first of July hit, and the fiends were in full rotation. Malikie directed traffic as the dope packs moved faster by the minute.

"Yo' Mal, we got to re-up again, my nigga. This shit is going fast. They copping it by the bundles today," Whip said, leaning into Malikie's 1990 Honda Accord.

Malikie stared at the phone, dreading having to call Gooney for another order, but business was crazy and the money never waits for a hustler.

A Ducati motorcycle engine revved up loud behind them, making Malikie look up from the phone as he started to press the buttons.

"Who the fuck is this nigga?" Whip asked, tapping Malikie on the shoulder.

"Pull the heat, my nigga. I don't know who the fuck this is."

Whip pulled the Glock 9 from under his shirt and cocked it in the car as the tall, muscular figure approached, still wearing his helmet. Whip quickly pulled the gun out and stuck it in his stomach when he got close enough.

"Who the fuck are you, nigga? You must be crazy pulling up on this block like that. What the fuck do you want anyway? You better talk fast or hurry up and get on that bullshit bike and skate out of here."

Malikie watched everything without saying a word.

"I need to talk to Malikie," the man said, taking off his helmet, and staring Malikie in the face. "You might want to hurry up and put that pistol up, before you hurt yourself."

Malikie smiled when he saw Jason standing before him, calm as ever.

"Aye cuz, dude is cool. Put that up before you do some dumb shit."

Whip mugged Jason as he tucked the Glock back under his shirt and stepped aside. Malikie sat up in his seat, as Whip stood close behind Jason, prepared for anything.

"You're Gooney's folks right?" Malikie asked.

Jason nodded his head as he leaned into the window.

"You ain't here to try and enforce some shit are you? My man back there will take your head off if you even flinch."

Jason glanced over his shoulder at Whip waiting patiently for any sign to fire. "I like the way you got your people ready, but, you can tell him to take a walk. I came to talk business."

Malikie looked him over for a second, noticing he didn't flinch or even act like he came for trouble.

"Whip, go make sure everything is being run right. I'ma hit you in a second."

"You sure, blood? I don't trust this nigga."

"It's cool, blood. Cuz don't want no problems. I think he way smarter than that."

Whip nodded his head and took off down the block.

"Can I get in?" Jason asked.

Malikie nodded his head, and Jason jumped in the passenger side. Malikie watched the block in silence as Jason stared out at the activity.

"You miss this, huh?" Malikie said, breaking the ice.

"Not at all. Some people are greedy and want everything out of the game. That's when you get fucked by the game. I got my piece and I'm cool with that."

"Then what you want with me?"

"How are things going with Goon? Are you eating right?"

"I'm eating, but on the real, I ain't feeling that nigga. He act like the world is his and nobody helped him get there. How the hell did you deal with that?"

Jason sighed, thinking about the old times him and Gooney had when they started out.

"Gooney used to be the most upstanding loyal type of cat you could ever meet. Money changes niggas who ain't ready for it. The fame and all the other traps, a man can get drunk off of. What are you in it for?"

"Money. Nothing more, nothing less! I don't care about any of the bitches or the other things that come with it. All I want is money and respect from the people I put on. I run things cool down here. That's why Goon put me on, but I just don't respect that nigga. He too dumb."

Jason smiled as a cop car pulled onto the street. All the hustlers handed their bundles to the lookout boys riding up and down the street on their bikes.

"I had a feeling you were about your business the day I met you. You wanted to do a smart move and Goon was running off of ego."

"Exactly, that's why I say I don't respect him. Fuck a ego! What we do is not about that in any way."

"So if you had control, you would run things a lot different?"

"No doubt! I know what to do. All I need is the connect."

"Ok, what if I told you I got a connect for you?"

"I would ask you what you want from me. Are you trying to step in Goon's place?

"Naw, not at all. I believe the wrong niggas have too much power, and they are fucking up what I started. All this right here would be very different if I never stepped in. Donovan ran it cool, but he fell to the evils in the game. I see you having your money already and you still being you, so I think you would do things different, but are you really ready to control all of it?"

"I don't even need to think about it. I know I'm ready for it all. Why you coming at me with this?"

"It's time for a new day. In order to grow, you have to get rid of the old weeds. So I need you to do one thing, and it's all yours."

"Get rid of Gooney, huh?"

"How did you know?"

"How could I not know? You're trying to give me basically a gold mine, and you don't want anything from it. What did he do to you?"

Jason thought back to the last words Chico said before he killed him.

"Never try to bite the hand that feeds you. That's all you need to know."

Malikie nodded his head in agreement. Jason secretly wished he had the time to do his dirty work, but not having any ties to a murder is the best way he could play it.

"I have to get out of here. As soon as that's done, let me know, and you will have a connect."

"How do I get in touch with you?"

"Don't worry," Jason said getting out of the car. "I will know about it as soon as it happens, then I will get in touch with you."

Chapter 30

Tanya sat in the back of the crowded superior courtroom in Hayward. It had been eight months since Donovan's attack on her and Italy, and Tanya wanted to see him sentenced to all the time he could possibly get. Families of other inmates took up the majority of the room, as women of all races held children and waited for the verdicts of their loved ones. Tanya texted Italy one more time, to see if she was coming. With no response after five minutes, she put her phone in her purse and waited for Donovan's case to come up.

Lawyers crowded the front of the room while an old white male judge sat high up on the stand, going through cases like water as he gave verdicts and put off cases for months. "Case number 4854692, the state of California versus Donovan Green," the court reporter yelled out.

Donovan came out of a back room chained around the waist, and connected to his wrists and around his ankles. Led by a well-built sheriff, Donovan scanned the room as he staggered slowly to stand next to his high paid lawyer. Tanya slid down in the seat as Donovan turned around to look into the crowd of eyes for a familiar face. Locking eyes with Tanya, Donovan let a smile creep across his face as the prosecutor proceeded.

"Your honor, Mr. Green is a danger to society and any one around him. He was found beating a woman to the verge of death. If police officers had not arrived in time, this would be a murder case instead of battery and assault." The District Attorney, a tiny Mexican woman, stood in front of a long cherry wood table, waving her hands at Donovan as she spoke the words she hoped would keep him incarcerated.

Donovan looked at the floor as she went on about the night of the attack. Slowly, he looked up at the huge seal of California hanging boldly behind the judge.

"Your honor," his lawyer chimed in. there is no reason to hold my client any further. This is the first time he has been in any trouble, and the victim was attempting to steal from him. My client merely reacted how any of us would, just in pure reaction and defense. We're not asking for the case to be thrown out, but just for the right to bail."

Donovan's lawyer placed his smooth bronze hand on Donovan's back as he spoke. His tailored suit made him look more like a mobster than a lawyer as he looked over his gold Gucci frames. The D.A. stared at his razor sharp lined Caesar as he spoke with charisma and charm. The judge nodded his head with every word, and Tanya knew what was coming.

"Ok Mr. Henderson, that's enough. We get the message," the judge said. After a second of looking at Donovan, he leaned back in his seat. "Ok, bail set at $100,000. We will convene here again in two months on June 12th. Next case!"

Donovan shook his lawyer's hand as he looked back at Tanya. She shook her head as she stood up to leave.

"Man, handle the bail for me, and I promise I will get you back the money as soon as I touch down," Donovan said before the bulky sheriff escorted him back into the building.

Mr. Henderson nodded his head as he shut his Gucci briefcase.

Donovan smiled once more as he locked eyes with Tanya.

He winked at her and kissed the air smiling again as Tanya looked on enraged. Donovan never broke his cold, vicious, devilish stare letting Tanya know that it was far from over between them. Everything seemed to be a fast blur as he disappeared through the door he came in; vengeance the first and only option his mind focused on.

Once in the hallway, Tanya dialed Italy's number again, hoping to get her on the line. Italy's phone went directly to voicemail, making Tanya more upset than she already was.

"Italy, the nigga is getting out on bail. You need to call me as soon as you get this message." Tanya said before slamming the flip phone.

"Fuck you, Jason Wright. Look how you have me. I can't even see my damn feet. My titties hurt every day. I can't take this."

Jason tried not to smile as he listened to Sheila complain about her bloated body. The baby was due any day, and Jason couldn't wait to hear silence from Sheila's mouth. She started crying miserably, and Jason wrapped his arms around her and brought her head down to his chest.

"Our baby is going to be real cute," Sheila said.

Jason laughed to himself. "Shit, cute is for puppies. Our baby is coming out a man."

"What makes you think our baby is going to be a boy?"

Jason shrugged. "I just know. We have a linebacker in there."

Sheila sat up and started laughing as she wiped her eyes. Jason thumbed a few tears away as he caressed her face. "You're beautiful, you know that? Even more now than before."

Sheila smacked her lips. "Stop it, Jay, you're making me blush and you know that is hard for a black woman to do. Well, Mr. Wright, are you ready for this?"

"Do I have a choice?" Jason said.

"Hell naw," Sheila said, struggling to get up. "You can try

that leaving me shit if you want to. You can't stop a bullet."

"Damn! Now you're talking about killing me? I can't wait until you drop this baby, because you have been tripping lately."

Sheila shouted from the kitchen. "I'm just saying, Jay. They say things change when the baby comes into play. Mainly with the male, because the things we used to do, don't get done too much anymore."

Jason sighed. "You need to stop listening to that lady on Oprah. That shit is for white folks. We've built our love together, and we shall continue to. We just have an extra head in the picture."

"Well what do you see us doing different?" Sheila asked.

"Just more family stuff. I don't want any weed puffing around him. Plus, we have to keep a camera with us at all times. I want his every move immortalized. That's something my momma didn't do too much with me. I barely have any baby flicks."

Sheila's face became somber. "Do you wish she was still here?"

Jason took a deep breath. "Of course, every day. I do even more, now. I wish her and my pops were here. I don't even know who my grandparents are. It's crazy how cycles repeat themselves. The same things our parents went through, we have to go through. Now my son has to grow up without any grandparents. Bino and Trisha are as close as he'll get."

Sheila sat down next to him. "I was thinking about our mothers last night. I don't want to make the same mistakes they did, having no direction when they lost our fathers. That's one reason I stay on you so much. I know I'd be crazy without you. I'd bounce back because that's what we do, but I wouldn't be the same. Jason, do you ever think I'd leave you?"

Jason started to laugh. "Hell naw! I put this dick on you too good."

Sheila shoved him as she giggled. "Well you ain't getting

any more of this. No, no. I'm not going through this shit again. Hella people were laughing at me waddling through the mall yesterday. I told Trisha right then, that you weren't getting any more of this."

"Well, you'll miss it more than me."

Sheila rolled her eyes. "Yeah right! Have you figured out what you're going to write about yet?"

Jason rubbed his forehead. "I don't know where to start. I thought about relationships, but that's overrated. Then I thought about this situation with Sav. That'll make a good book, but that situation isn't over yet. I've been thinking about driving down there to see what's going on with him, but I'm not ready for that. I might end up slapping the hell out of him. That's the only thing I hate about money. It can make blood turn on blood. It's hard enough for black folks to really get it, with the police and Feds all over the place, but then you have to worry about the ones closest to you.

"My momma told me this might happen. That's why I always try to stay low key. I never thought it would hit with me and my own brother. My momma told me it was going to happen with Gooney, though. I think if me and Sav both had guns on us at that time, we would've drawn."

Sheila shook her head. "Jason you have to let that play out. Remember that time you and Sav got in that fight at Linda's barbeque? We couldn't break you two up for nothing. You two carry so much built up anger that it makes both of you crazy. I think you're mad at him because that's what you used to be, and he's mad at you because you're what he wants to be. That's why he always brings up the things you have. Let him live and blow up his ego. It'll come down, and then he will be back."

Jason kissed her on the forehead. "Why do you always know what to say?"

Sheila held his face in hers. "Because I'm your other half. I told you, God made us at the same time."

Jason got up from the couch and helped her up. "You

want to dance with me?"

He pressed play on the stereo and Maxwell's smooth voice came over the speakers. Jason moved behind Sheila and wrapped his arms around her waist. He rubbed his hands all over her stomach as he kissed her neck.

"Mmmmm, Jay that feels good." Shelia said as they swayed slowly to the music. Sheila suddenly jerked forward, holding her stomach. She felt a wetness dripping down her legs. "Jay, it's time. My water just broke."

Jason stood back and looked at her. "Are you sure?"

Sheila yelled back at him. "Yeah I'm sure, nigga."

Jason sat down with his mouth open and his eyes bugged out.

"Jason, get your black ass up," she said, breathing heavily. "This kid is ready. He's kicking the hell out of me. Jason, get the fuck up!"

Jason jumped to his feet and then went searching for Sheila's hospital bag.

"Jay, it's already by the door," Sheila said, holding her stomach.

Jason grabbed the bag and ran to the car, forgetting about everything he needed to do, especially helping Sheila to the door. Sheila stood at the door, frowning and cussing him out as he ran to escort her to the car.

"Jay, slow down baby. I'm the one running through hell with gasoline draws on. All you have to do is be cool. Please don't drive all crazy to get to the hospital."

Jason ushered her into the car, rolling his eyes as Sheila cursed between breaths. Sheila screamed as Jason pulled into traffic. She grabbed his thigh and squeezed hard, making Jason shriek out in pain as he almost crashed into a stop sign, trying to pry his leg loose. Sheila let his leg go and continued breathing hard.

"Owwww!" Jason said, waiting at a red light. "What was that for?"

Sheila grabbed her stomach. "That was a contraction, baby. I needed something to grab and squeeze. This boy is kicking hard. He's ready."

The light turned green, and Jason screeched into the intersection. "Jay, slow the hell down! You gone get us pulled over before we even get to the hospital," Sheila yelled.

"Hell naw. You aren't going to keep squeezing my leg like that," Jason said as the car finally swerved into the emergency section at Manteca Medical. Jason started to run inside, but saw two ambulance drivers coming towards him. He stopped them as they came outside, hoping to get some immediate help. "I got a pregnant woman out here. She's ready to bust."

"I'm sorry buddy," one of them said. "We just got off. Try the receptionist."

Jason grabbed the man by the arm and began slapping him in the back of the head. "This is your fucking job, man. Now get over there and help my wife into the emergency room," he screamed, slapping the driver repeatedly as he ushered him to the car. Jason opened the door as Sheila was going through another contraction.

"Jay, give me your hand, baby," she said, reaching out for him.

"Hell naw," Jason said, stepping back. "What are y'all waiting for? Help her out."

The two men helped her out of the car. One disappeared into the hospital and returned with a wheelchair.

"All right, ma'am, I need you to sit here in this chair and put your feet on the foot rest. We're going to take care of you now."

Jason helped her down into the chair and stood back quickly. Sheila shot him a cold look as the ambulance driver pushed her into the hospital.

The driver that Jason slapped stood at the entrance with a nurse. Jason looked at the redhead lady in amusement. "Anybody ever told you that you look like Mrs. Garrett from the Facts of Life?" he said.

The old lady laughed. "What is your name, sir?"

"My name is Jason Wright, and this is my wife, Sheila. She's about to explode and we need a doctor fast."

The nurse shook her head. "Okay, I'm going to need-"

Jason cut her off before she could start. "We have insurance, lady. Now please help us." The lady stood in shock. "I see. Okay, we'll put her in 2104 and I'll be right there. Mr. Wright, I'm going to have to ask you to stay back and fill out these forms."

"I'll fill them out later. I'm staying with my wife right now."

"Well, if you don't fill out the forms, the doctors won't see her. Now which do you want?"

Sheila grabbed his leg and squeezed it hard as the two paramedics laughed.

Jason screamed out in pain. "Okay damn! Where are the papers at?" The old woman handed him a clipboard as she moved behind the paramedics. Jason sat down as he heard Sheila screaming down the hallway.

"You have a beautiful wife," a slender white woman said, holding her infant son.

"Thank you," he replied.

The woman sat down next to him as he started filling out the forms. "I also think what you did to make them help you was totally in the right. These fuckers here are so lazy. They really won't help you unless you have insurance. My husband had to drive back home just to get the medical card."

Jason stopped what he was doing. "Oh my God, thank you. I almost forgot everything," he said, jumping up and running out of the hospital.

His car was still parked illegally in front of the hospital with the doors open. He parked the car and returned with Sheila's hospital bags. Quickly, he filled the papers out, showed identification and proof of insurance, and then ran to Sheila's room. A doctor and a nurse were now with her and timing her contractions. Sheila began screaming again, hollering Jason's name.

"Five minutes doctor," the nurse said, timing Sheila's contractions.

"Is she prepped?" The doctor asked, turning to Jason. "Sir, how long has she been contracting?"

Jason shrugged as he looked at Sheila's sweaty body. The doctor snapped Jason out of his trance. "Well, Mr. Wright, it seems she's been in labor now for a couple of hours."

Jason looked confused. "That can't be. Her water just broke."

The doctor shook his head. "That usually happens several hours into labor. Her contractions are getting closer together. Anyhow, we need you to suit up and try to calm Sheila down as much as possible. Did you two take Lamaze classes?"

Jason slowly nodded his head.

"Okay," the doctor said. "Then you know what to do. I'll return in a few minutes to check her progress." The doctor walked out of the room as Sheila lay in the bed, breathing so hard, he thought she would fall off the bed.

"Jay, come here, baby." Jason rushed to her side, taking her hands in his. "We're about to have a baby, Jay. Our baby! I love you so much."

Jason kissed her forehead. "I love you too. I can't believe this is happening. It's all so crazy. The cold part is you're still the most beautiful woman in the world."

"Oh baby, thank you," she said, kissing his lips. "But I look like shit and you know it."

Shelia then screamed from another contraction as she squeezed Jason's hand, making him holler out in pain again. She slowly let go as the contraction calmed.

"Jason, I'm going to kill you for putting me through this. This is all your fault. I hate you! Oh, I hate you so much! Get the fuck out of my room!"

Jason stared at Sheila's blazing fury and walked slowly out of the room.

A nurse handed him his garb and checked his hand. "You'll be all right. Nothing is sprained or broken. She just gave you a good squeeze. Listen, she means nothing she's saying right now. This is normal in delivery. She really needs you in there right now."

Jason thanked the nurse and walked to a payphone to call Bino. After informing him of what was going on, Jason sat on a bench outside of the room to gather himself and focus on the happiness he was experiencing.

Chapter 31

"Girl, look at you, you look terrible. I have to get flicks of this, because you might not ever look this bad again in your life," Trisha said as she began taking pictures of Sheila.

Jason and Bino sat in the corner of the room conversing quietly.

"You know your life is about to change forever? I still think you two should've waited, but I am happy for the both of you. You have a lot of knowledge under your belt, and you can teach this child all of it."

Jason ran his hand over his head. "Bee, did you ever think about whether or not you'd be a good father?"

Bino laughed. "Of course. When we had our first, I didn't know how I was going to do this. I knew Trisha would be a good mother, because she's good at running the house and taking care of people. Plus, she's a teacher. But I didn't know how I would be. What I've learned, Jay, is that you can't plan anything out with parenting. It will never go the way you planned. All you can do is pray for the best, and be the best parent you can be. You can obey all the parenting laws there are, but you will still have drama raising them.

"Kids grow up and they go through things. A lot of the shit will piss you off, but you still have to love and support them to the fullest. My advice is to remember that you were a child once. Try to relate to them at all times, and try not to be overbearing, but, don't let them run over you. Play the good guy, and let Sheila be the mean one. She's good at that."

Jason smiled. "I just hope things don't change too much between me and Sheila. We have a lot of fun, but I know all good things one day come to an end.

"Jay, women don't get tired of these things. They have a yearning for family life. It all depends on you. How you maintain and carry yourself. You'll get tired before she does. Regular life can be boring as hell. You never had problems before, because you were in the game, but now it will be work, home, and fussing. A lot of headache that a man has to be prepared for."

Jason smirked. "So is that why you are still in this?"

Bino was silent as he contemplated an answer. "No. I have my own reasons, but that is not it. If you ever have to get back in, you'll understand. As a matter of fact, you'll call me with the same reasons."

Jason stared at Sheila's stomach. He thought about his father and wondered if this is how he felt when his mother was giving birth.

Sheila suddenly screamed out Jason's name. Everyone jumped up and rushed to her side. "It's time now, baby. He's coming out noooooowwwwww."

"Call the doctor in here, Bee," Jason said, holding her hand.

Bino and Trisha rushed to get the doctor while Jason held Sheila in his arms as everyone came into the room.

The doctors and nurses took their positions. "Okay Mr. Wright, this baby is coming out now. She is fully dilated 10 cm, so let's get this child into the world."

Bino and Trisha walked out of the room to the waiting area. The doctor put his head between Sheila's legs. "Okay Sheila, I need you to push with all your might. Give it all you got."

Sheila held Jason's hand as she began pouring sweat,

screaming and pushing until she could do no more. "Okay," the doctor said. "We have a head. Give me another push, Sheila." Sheila repeated the process.

"That's right, baby. You're doing good, sweetie," Jason said, kissing her forehead.

The doctor looked up at her. "Now Sheila, if you give me one more good push, this child will be free. Can you do that for me?"

"You can do it, baby," Jason whispered in her ear.

Sheila nodded her head at the doctor, trying her hardest to gather the strength to push with all her might as she squeezed Jason's hand with everything she had.

"All right, we have a winner," the doctor said, holding the baby in his hands. "It's a boy," the doctor said. "Jason? Would you like to cut the umbilical cord?"

Jason thought about it and declined, while holding Sheila in his arms as the nurses took care of the baby.

He kissed Sheila on the cheek. "You did it, ma. We're parents, baby. We have a beautiful son. He's so big. Look how beautiful he is," he whispered as the nurses took the baby for examination.

Sheila lay panting, gripping Jason's hand in hers.

"He's quiet, Jay. He's just like you already." Jason rubbed her on the forehead and kissed her lips.

Sheila suddenly felt light headed.

"Jay, I don't feel right. I'm so tired," she said, jerking her head up to keep it from falling.

"What's up, ma?"

Sheila struggled to sit up. "I don't know. I feel so weak."

Jason quickly darted his eyes up and down her body. "Maybe you're supposed to. You just spent like five hours in labor. Just relax, baby."

Sheila closed her eyes and didn't move.

"Sheila? Sheila?" Jason called out to her.

Sheila didn't move or respond.

"Nurse, my wife isn't moving," Jason said in a panic.

The nurse smiled as she turned around to check on her. Her smile faded when she checked between her legs and then her pupils before running out of the room, leaving him alone with his unresponsive wife.

"Baby, wake up," Jason said shaking her.

Sheila didn't move.

The doctors rushed into the room with an extra gurney, moving him out of the way.

The doctor continued checking all her signs. "Okay everyone, she's lost a lot of blood. It looks like her placenta disconnected before the baby came. She's hemorrhaging badly right now. We have to get her to the operating room immediately. Mr. Wright, I'm going to have to ask you to wait in the lobby. We'll be out to inform you shortly."

Jason tried rushing to Sheila's side, but was grabbed by two male nurses.

"Mr. Wright, I need you to keep your cool now, and let us do our job. Your wife has lost a lot of blood, and the only thing that matters right now is trying to save her life. So I need you to keep your cool, please."

Jason stood aside and watched as they wheeled Sheila out of the room. Her face looked as if she was sleeping peacefully as Jason stood by, not knowing if the few moments after she gave birth to their child would be the last time he would ever get to speak to her.

He followed the medical crew out of the room and watched them rush down the hall. Jason looked up to the ceiling as he slid down the wall and put his face in his hands, praying silently for the curse of death to skip over the last and only woman he ever loved.

PART 2 COMING SOON!
2 Sides of a Penny
Part 2 on the way!
@carlbdreamkings

Want more #hot #fiction and #nonfiction titles?
www.lifechangingbooks.net

CHECK OUT THE OTHER NEW RELEASES AND BOOKS AVAILABLE FOR PRE-ORDER!

A WIFE'S BETRAYAL
BY MISS KP

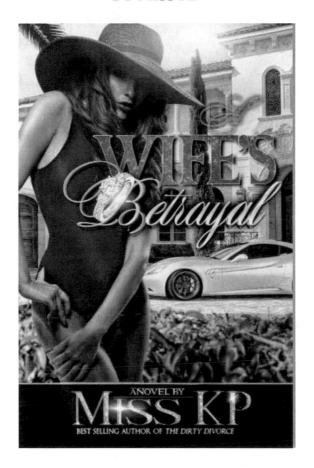

TISHA RAYE'S DEBUT NOVEL
KING AND QUEEN!

D. HENDERSON'S DEBUT NOVEL
CAREER CRIMINAL
AVAILABLE FOR PRE-ORDER!

AVERY GOODE'S
PILLOW PRINCESS
PART 1 AND 2!

BEST-SELLING AUTHOR KENDALL BANKS DOES IT
AGAIN WITH *FILTHY RICH* PART 1 AND 2!
PART 3 IS ON THE WAY!
@authorkendallb

DANETTE MAJETTE PRESENTS
I SHOULDA SEEN HIM COMIN' PART 1 AND 2!
GET IT NOW ONLY ON KINDLE!
@DCMAJETTE

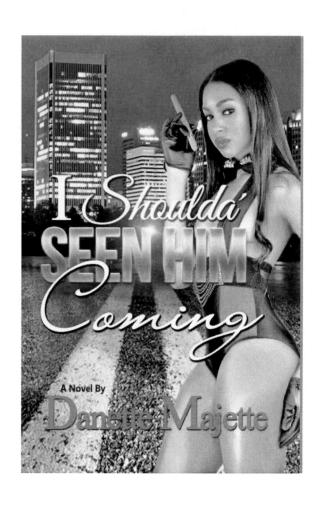

LCB BOOK TITLES

See More Titles At
www.lifechangingbooks.net

PAPARAZZI

A NOVEL BY

MISS KP

BEST SELLING AUTHOR OF TH

The Dirty Divorce Part 3

A NOVEL BY

MISS KP

In STORES Now

www.lifechangingbooks.net

ORDER FORM

MAIL TO:
PO Box 423
Brandywine, MD 20613
301-362-6508

Ship to:	
Address:	.
City & State:	Zip:

Date: _____ Phone: _____
Email: _____

Make all money orders and cashiers checks payable to: **Life Changing Books**

Qty.	ISBN	Title	Release Date	Price
	0-9741394-2-4	Bruised by Azarel	Jul-05	$ 15.00
	0-9741394-7-5	Bruised 2: The Ultimate Revenge by Azarel	Oct-06	$ 15.00
	0-9741394-3-2	Secrets of a Housewife by J. Tremble	Feb-06	$ 15.00
	0-9741394-6-7	The Millionaire Mistress by Tiphani	Nov-06	$ 15.00
	1-934230-99-5	More Secrets More Lies by J. Tremble	Feb-07	$ 15.00
	1-934230-95-2	A Private Affair by Mike Warren	May-07	$ 15.00
	1-934230-96-0	Flexin & Sexin Volume 1	Jun-07	$ 15.00
	1-934230-89-8	Still a Mistress by Tiphani	Nov-07	$ 15.00
	1-934230-91-X	Daddy's House by Azarel	Nov-07	$ 15.00
	1-934230-88-X	Naughty Little Angel by J. Tremble	Feb-08	$ 15.00
	1-934230820	Rich Girls by Kendall Banks	Oct-08	$ 15.00
	1-934230839	Expensive Taste by Tiphani	Nov-08	$ 15.00
	1-934230782	Brooklyn Brothel by C. Stecko	Jan-09	$ 15.00
	1-934230669	Good Girl Gone bad by Danette Majette	Mar-09	$ 15.00
	1-934230804	From Hood to Hollywood by Sasha Raye	Mar-09	$ 15.00
	1-934230707	Sweet Swagger by Mike Warren	Jun-09	$ 15.00
	1-934230677	Carbon Copy by Azarel	Jul-09	$ 15.00
	1-934230723	Millionaire Mistress 3 by Tiphani	/ Nov-09	$ 15.00
	1-934230715	A Woman Scorned by Ericka Williams	Nov-09	$ 15.00
	1-934230685	My Man Her Son by J. Tremble	Feb-10	$ 15.00
	1-924230731	Love Heist by Jackie D.	Mar-10	$ 15.00
	1-934230812	Flexin & Sexin Volume 2	Apr-10	$ 15.00
	1-934230748	The Dirty Divorce by Miss KP	May-10	$ 15.00
	1-934230758	Chedda Boyz by CJ Hudson	Jul-10	$ 15.00
	1-934230766	Snitch by VegasClarke	Oct-10	$ 15.00
	1-934230693	Money Maker by Tonya Ridley	Oct-10	$ 15.00
	1-934230774	The Dirty Divorce Part 2 by Miss KP	Nov-10	$ 15.00
	1-934230170	The Available Wife by Carla Pennington	Jan-11	$ 15.00
	1-934230774	One Night Stand by Kendall Banks	Feb-11	$ 15.00
	1-934230278	Bitter by Danette Majette	Feb-11	$ 15.00
	1-934230299	Married to a Balla by Jackie D.	May-11	$ 15.00
	1-934230308	The Dirty Divorce Part 3 by Miss KP	Jun-11	$ 15.00
	1-934230316	Next Door Nympho By CJ Hudson	Jun-11	$ 15.00
	1-934230286	Bedroom Gangsta by J. Tremble	Sep-11	$ 15.00
	1-934230340	Another One Night Stand by Kendall Banks	Oct-11	$ 15.00
	1-934230359	The Available Wife Part 2 by Carla Pennington	Nov-11	$ 15.00
	1-934230332	Wealthy & Wicked by Chris Renee	Jan-12	$ 15.00
	1-934230375	Life After a Balla by Jackie D.	Mar-12	$ 15.00
	1-934230251	V.I.P. by Azarel	Apr-12	$ 15.00
	1-934230383	Welfare Grind by Kendall Banks	May-12	$ 15.00
	1 934230413	Still Grindin' by Kendall Banks	Sep-12	$ 15.00
	1-934230391	Paparazzi by Miss KP	Oct-13	$ 15.00
	1-93423043X	Cashin' Out by Jai Nicole	Nov-12	$ 15.00
	1-934230634	Welfare Grind Part 3 by Kendall Banks		$15.00
	1-934230642	Game Over by Winter Ramos	Apr-13	$15.99
			Total for Books	**$**

* Prison Orders- Please allow up to three (3) weeks for delivery.	Shipping Charges (add $4.95 for 1-4 books*)	$
	Total Enclosed (add lines)	$

Please Note: We are not held responsible for returned prison orders. Make sure the facility will receive books before ordering.

*Shipping and Handling of 5-10 books is $6.95, please contact us if your order is more than 10 books. (301)362-6508

For More Book Titles Please Visit

www.lifechangingbooks.net

facebook.com/lifechangingbooks
Twitter: @lcbooks
Instagram:@lcbbooks